He spent the first  Vicodin. By the fourt_____, and he was able to eat at a nearby diner. His strength returned as soon as he had some solid food in him.

He kept up on the news. The killings were no longer the main story. Nobody cared about a bunch of dead East Europeans with criminal backgrounds. Outside the news, he tried to watch television, but the cable selection was limited. It was mostly newer movies, which he hated. To him, actors and entertainers were pretentious, overpaid dancing monkeys. The Greco Romans had the right idea when they made their entertainers fight it out to the death in Colosseums. He'd pay to watch that.

With nothing grabbing his interest, he stared at the ceiling. He would wait a while longer before he made his next move. He wasn't done with Sin City yet.

Farewell, Las Vegas

by

Grant Bywaters

Farewell, Las Vegas

Cover Art by *Rae Monet, Inc. Design*

The Wild Rose Press, Inc.
PO Box 708
Adams Basin, NY 14410-0708
Visit us at www.thewildrosepress.com

Publishing History
First Mainstream Thriller Edition, 2020
Print ISBN 978-1-5092-3055-6
Digital ISBN 978-1-5092-3056-3

Published in the United States of America

Dedication

For My Amazing Wife Heidy

Chapter 1

The Lucky Hearts Casino sat a few blocks from the Freemont Experience. A place for hardcore gamblers and those lured in by the cheaper slot machines but lower payouts.

Joe Roddick knew his way around when he walked in. He didn't even need to look to see where he was going. Instead, he aimlessly stared down at the ugly carpet all casinos seemed to have. Rumor was, it was designed to be such an eyesore that people had no choice but to keep their attention at the tables. Though Roddick had been told, the unsightly design was to hide the wear and tear from heavy foot traffic.

Roddick was middle-aged, with an average build, brown hair, and sharp, gray eyes. He was always ill-shaven, which seemed to match his uncouth demeanor.

Security knew Roddick well enough to allow him to make his way to the back unmolested. He continued down a back hallway and opened the door to a room full of television monitors and a desk. Sitting behind it was a middle-aged overweight man whose name plate read *Floyd Lockhart, Operations Manager.*

"Good to see you, Joe," Lockhart said, not bothering to get up.

"Likewise."

Roddick took the seat across from him, crossed his arms over his chest, and waited for Lockhart to finish stuffing the Krispy Kreme down his throat with the heel of his hand, so he could fill him in on why he was summoned.

Between licks of his fingers, Lockhart said, "Got an easy job for you."

"That so?"

"Yeah. Simple locate job."

Roddick grimaced. "Sorry, I'm not locating anyone for your loan shark pals again. Last time they sent the guy to the ER. Damn near lost my license."

"I remember. Don't worry about that this time."

"What's the job?"

"Just a cat that got lucky and left with a lot of house money. Naturally, we'd like to find him and see about luring him in here again so he can give it all back."

"How you goin' to do that? Offer him free tickets to Celine Dion?"

"That broad still playin' here? Shit, shows how much I pay attention. But no, he wouldn't be interested in that."

"A no-nonsense pro?"

Lockhart leaned back in his chair and interlocked his fingers across a bulging stomach.

"Somethin' like that. We were able to get his name from the ATM he used. Nick Rivera. Also printed a pic of him from the security cameras."

He handed Roddick a photocopy of a casino floor surveillance photo of Rivera. It was poor quality and the image was pixilated, blocky to the point it reminded Roddick of a character in the video game Minecraft. He was familiar with the game because his daughter liked to play it.

"Still haven't updated your surveillance system."

Lockhart groaned. "The way the casino sees it, why spend the money on that when they can get a couple more slot machines that can bring them in money."

The man in the picture looked to be 5'10 to 6'0, around 190 to 200 pounds, brown hair, and a long, narrow nose. That was about all Roddick could get from the printout. With nothing more to go on he stood up and said, "I'll see what I can do."

"That would be doing me a solid, Joe."

Roddick squinted. He could hear the desperation in Lockhart's voice.

"How much money did he walk out with?"

Lockhart waved his hands around trying to avoid answering, but Roddick waited.

"Let's just say over a million and leave it at that."

Chapter 2

From the Lucky Hearts Casino, Roddick drove to his office on Las Vegas Boulevard and Warm Spring Road, two or so miles south of the *Welcome to Fabulous Las Vegas* sign.

It was early January, and half the buildings and homes on the way still had their Christmas lights up. Having grown up in Providence, Rhode Island, seeing palm trees with lights on them never sat right with Roddick.

The place he was renting was in a small plaza, sandwiched between a donut shop and a dry cleaner. It was more of a meeting space than an actual office, since he did most of his work at home or on the road. It was all for the illusion of some sort of professionalism since most clients found meeting at coffee shops or at their residence to be on the shady side.

He hadn't been to it since the holidays and felt he might as well check in and get some use out of it to justify paying the rent. No sooner had he opened the door, he could smell the stale, unventilated air. He left the door ajar and took all the holiday junk mail crammed through his mail slot and dumped it in the trash without even bothering to look at it.

The room had a small conference table, some chairs, and a half-full water dispenser. Roddick set his laptop on the table and spent the remainder of the afternoon going through dozens of websites and databases searching for Nick Rivera. He scanned court databases and dockets, property records, public records, employment records, and even political contribution records for the hell of it. He got a few possible hits he would have to vet, but that would need to wait. Roddick checked his watch and saw that it was nearing six. His daughter would be coming soon.

****

The Scorpion came out of the jet bridge to the comforting sounds of jangly music and spinning wheels of the slot machines of McCarran Airport. He always enjoyed his visits to Vegas. A hedonistic wonderland. Someday he'd like to come when it didn't pertain to business.

He was slightly above average height, an athletic build, 'All-American' good looks, with short, spiky blondish hair, and cold, blue-gray eyes. His youthful face hid his actual age well.

His dress was smart casual with a lightweight blazer, a blue button Denim shirt, navy Chino pants, and plain leather sneakers. He looked like most middle-aged men going to business seminars or a weekend trip to the tables.

He checked his watch and saw that he had time. He was in no hurry. He had no luggage to claim, just carry-on. He browsed the rows of slots, steering clear of the video reel ones because they offered the lowest return. He found the one he liked, a classic three-reel slot called Ultimate 777, next to some old blue-haired woman you'd find at almost any casino.

He liked slots because they gave his always-working brain a rest. There was no strategy to them.

The random number generator chips they all ran off of made any kind of strategy impossible. You had about as much chance winning on your first spin as you would on your 650th. There was a beauty to that kind of randomness.

He played until he used up the credit he'd fed into it and moved on to a few other slots before he figured it was time to get on with it. Besides, if all went well, he'd be back here in a few days and could play some more before his flight out.

Chapter 3

"Your turn," Kaylee said.

Roddick chalked his cue stick and looked at his options. Like a lot of homes in the Vegas area, it came with a pool and poker table. Before Roddick bought the place, it used to be rented out until the neighbors had enough of drunken parties and shenanigans and forced the owners to put the house up to auction. Roddick got it for a steal.

"Combination, 5 into the 13 in the corner," he said.

He made his next three shots before potting the cue ball.

"You did that on purpose," she said.

"Can't prove it."

His flame-haired nineteen-year-old daughter was sharp. He'd realized that the first time she came into his life. That was when a familiar looking redhead named Linda walked into the Northern Providence Police Department and told him her ten-year-old daughter was not only his but that she needed his help.

Apparently, the fruit of his loins was an up and coming computer hacker. She had hacked into a few big operating systems so she could get free video games and was facing charges of technical burglary. He was able to get it dismissed on the condition she wasn't allowed on any devices unsupervised.

From that point on his involvement in her life was

limited. Especially when he turned a trip to Vegas, after getting suspended, into a permanent stay. The upshot, being the smart kid she was, she got offered scholarships to pretty much any college she wanted, and so she chose the University of Nevada, Las Vegas. The decision infuriated her mother, who knew it was only because of him.

"She could've gone to Harvard or Yale!" Linda yelled at him over the phone upon telling him his daughter would be moving to a dorm on the UNLV campus.

"If you think I had anything to do with this, you're wrong," he had told her. "I haven't talked to her in months."

Now, here she was, about to start her second semester next week after winter vacation. She'd flown back to Rhode Island to spend Christmas with Linda. She didn't want to, but Roddick insisted. Mainly because he didn't want to hear from Linda on how he was stealing her daughter away.

"Got any interesting cases you're working on?" Kaylee asked, while setting up her shot.

Roddick grabbed a chicken wing and shook his head. "Not at the moment."

"Let me know if you need my help."

By help, she meant computer-related. Her talent for hacking had only progressed from the time she was caught. It was now her lifelong ambition to be the female Julian Assange of WikiLeaks. While most girls her age would be out drinking and experimenting with drugs and boys, her idea of a good time was going through data dumps of classified government documents with her online buddies.

Her mother shunned it, but Roddick only encouraged it. Why not? His knowledge of computers and all things digital were adequate but nothing compared to the youth of today. Besides, she jailbroke his Firestick so he could watch pretty much any show or movie he wanted.

"I might just take you up on that offer," he said.

She sank her next two shots but scratched her third. "You thought about me moving in with you next semester?"

Roddick scowled. "I don't think your mother would like that very much."

"Doesn't matter. I'm nineteen."

"Won't stop her from harassing me every day. Besides, don't you want to be with kids your own age?"

Kaylee laughed. "They all just want to party and hang out on the Strip. Not my thing."

"No, your thing is trying to crack the Pentagon's firewall with your cyber buddies."

Roddick sank his last ball, leaving him only the eight.

"You know me too well," she said. "Mom says I'm too much like you. I don't know how she would know that considering you two were never together for any real length of time."

It was true. Her conception was the after-effects of too much booze with a redheaded lawyer he met at a legal seminar. Though there was a strong attraction between the two, there was nothing else. They were two very different people.

"You know the paradox of what happens when an unstoppable force meets an immovable object? Well, that's your mother and I, but I'll let you figure out which one is which."

"You're the unstoppable force, obviously."

"You sure about that?" he asked, putting the eight away in the side pocket.

"Pretty sure," she said. "Are we still going to the hockey game next week?"

The Boston Bruins were coming to play the Vegas Golden Knights next Saturday, and Roddick had made sure to get tickets. He was a lifelong Bruins fan.

One of his earliest memories was watching them on TV as the entire team climbed into the stands of Madison Square Garden to brawl it out with spectators. The minute he saw Bruins defenseman Mike Milbury beating a New York fan with his own shoe, he was hooked.

"Yes, unless you'd rather not go."

Her eyes widened. "Of course, I want to go. I was just thinking of what I should wear."

"Oh, about that." Roddick hooked their cues back on the wall and left the room. He came back a moment later carrying a folded-up jersey.

"You can wear this."

Kaylee grabbed it and let the black and yellow jersey hang down.

"Oh, geez, Dad, you shouldn't have."

"I can take it back if you don't like it."

"No, no. I do."

Confused as to whether or not she was being sincere, Roddick took her at her word and got up to grab another beer. For someone who didn't like her mother, she sure acted like her at times.

****

The Scorpion flipped through channels paying no

attention to the man lying on the couch with the dead white eyes staring up at the ceiling. A small amount of blood seeped from the hole in the center of his head.

It was an easy job, for being so rushed. The only complication came with the car rental. The Scorpion had started using rentals a while back because stolen cars were reported and spotted faster with so much surveillance around these days. With a rental, the car had local plates with a clean tag that would slip by security cameras. He had plenty of fake IDs, and rental companies never did much to verify.

It was a perfect system, until yesterday. He had ordered a boring older model Corolla. Something that would fit in and not be given a second thought. That was not the car waiting for him in the space he was told to pick it up in the garage. What was parked in the given spot was a new-model beige Dodge Challenger.

He told the man he had checked in with at the counter there must have been a mistake, but the attendant said it wasn't.

"No, I did you a solid, buddy. I upgraded you. No extra charge."

Annoyed, the Scorpion argued against the upgrade, but this only seemed to draw suspicion from the rental people. It wasn't often a young male with no wife or kids didn't want a fancier car.

"Fucking Vegas," the Scorpion cursed as he punched the V-8 engine and peeled out of the rental garage.

He was in luck that in this town, flashy cars were a dime a dozen and locals seemed to be desensitized to it all. Nobody gave him a second look when he pulled into the apartment address he was given and waited.

The man he was looking for came out of a room and got into a beat-up Honda with expired plates.

He reversed out fast causing the Honda to fishtail as the tires grabbed on with what little tread they had left and stabled out as he put the car into drive and left. He'd be back soon enough, and the Scorpion would be waiting for him.

The lock to the place was easy to pick. Most door locks were useless to begin with. False sense of security was what they were. The place was a small, around 450 square feet, one-bedroom affair. There was minimum furniture. A couch and La-Z-Boy in the living area and a single bed without a frame in the closet-size bedroom.

That's where he was when he heard the door opening forty minutes later.

His target was still clutching a pizza box when the Scorpion stepped in front of him, stuck a 9mm to his forehead and fired. He was able to grab the pizza and the man, to keep him from falling to the ground and making noise.

He tossed the man, who had a frozen stunned expression on his face, on the couch and checked the windows. It was closing in on five and cars were pulling into the parking lot. People were getting home from work. A group of teens were hanging out in front of some wannabe-thug's GTO.

The Scorpion would wait it out until it died down. Over-cautious, maybe. But he didn't need that one bored neighbor getting a good look at him. Besides, it was these types of precautions that kept him from being caught.

Not letting a good pizza go to waste, he sat in the La-Z-Boy and started flipping through channels until he got to a history one showing a documentary on the Battle for Hill 937 aka Hamburger Hill. It was a battle that summed up the entire Vietnam War. Sending men through a meat grinder of enemy and friendly fire to take the hill that had no strategic value, only to give it back to the gooks days later. The decision didn't surprise the Scorpion. The military was full of idiots being put into positions of authority.

It was the biggest reason why his stint in the armed forces didn't last as long as he originally intended. Though killing had always come naturally to him, caring about the well-being of the men in his unit did not. Nor did taking orders from men who were mentally inferior to him.

He was able to fake them all into believing he was conforming to the military way of life, but little by little the men in his unit saw glimpses of who he really was. They saw first-hand in the Middle East how little their lives meant to him as one by one they fell. Why should he have cared? They were all weak. He saw the fear in their eyes as they went into enemy fire.

Things started to come to a head when his unit came under scrutiny after a five-day fire fight with Islamic insurgents in a mountain village inside the Kunar Province that ended with heavy civilian casualties. Shortly after that, he got into an off-duty fight with a fellow officer that ended with the Scorpion almost ripping the man's jaw completely off. He got court-martialed and sentenced to a reduction in rank and time in the brig. His military career was essentially over from that point on.

He glanced at his phone. Past six. He turned the TV off and dropped the half-eaten pizza into the box on the dead man's chest before letting himself out.

Chapter 4

Roddick drained most of the day doing insurance fraud cases, which was a bulk of what he did. He'd just closed out a big one that had the cops helping out. An organized car crash scheme where two of them in separate cars would get in front of a victim and slam on their brakes, forcing the victim to rear end them. Roddick picked up on it when multiple insurance companies were sending him cases with identical situations.

It was late afternoon before Roddick was free to start going through and crossing off the several Nick Riveras he found.

The first was a senior citizen in a shoddy home on West Flamingo Road. The other was a juvenile around seventeen years old, living with his mom. Roddick assumed the kid was some delinquent because before he could say anything, the mom swung the door open and asked what he had done this time.

The third was a dead end. The address he had ended up being a drive-through ATM. It must have been recent because the ATM wasn't showing up on the mapping portal on his phone. In Vegas, that wasn't uncommon. The city was around-the-clock construction. Buildings and sites were constantly getting torn down and new ones being built in their place in a matter of weeks.

The last name Roddick had was at some low-income apartment complex on Cambridge Street in the Southeast part of town. It was an older complex built in Googie architecture with its exaggerated angles, bold colors, and atomic/ futuristic design.

The flashing starburst-lit sign read Holiday Apartments. Judging from the parked heaps on their last set of wheels and shoddy neighborhood, Roddick guessed most of the tenants were on some form of government assistance.

Roddick had found the address from a small auto loan Rivera had applied for and was denied two months prior. Chances were, he had probably moved out. People that occupied places like these never stayed long. That was the point.

He opened his glove box and took out a flyer to the Rockabilly Weekend at the Orleans. He checked the time on his dash. It was nearing seven. Past any kind of respectable hour to be leaving a flyer. Then again, it wasn't exactly a respectable area either.

Room 407 was on the third floor overlooking the pool. Roddick rapped on the door a few times to no response. Out of old habit, he hugged the doorway and tried the knob. Unlocked. The place was dark as Roddick stepped in. Using the flashlight from his phone, he lit his way through the small entrance that went into the meager living area. He was hoping to find a picture or something that would confirm it was the person he was looking for.

What he found instead was the man in the pixilated photo lying face up on his couch with a pizza box on his chest.

Roddick had seen a lot of dead bodies through his

career as a cop. Some in the worst condition imaginable. Those never bothered him. The more gruesome and excessive the death meant there was passion involved. A vengeful lover. A spited friend. Any time you heard of a vic being stabbed 72 times you knew it was coming from a place of deep, intense, emotion.

This was not that. It was emotionless. The cold-blooded execution-type kill always got to him. He knew that was what he was looking at because not far from the body was a Glock 9mm. With a heavy sigh, he knew he was in for a long night as he called it in.

****

People became police officers for many reasons. Some did it for the power over others; some did it because they really do feel they could make a difference. Over time, those reasons faded into a dull cloud of cynicism. But one thing that stayed constant was the sense of belonging to the brotherhood you'd joined the minute you put the blue uniform on.

Roddick knew all about the brotherhood. The "us versus them" mentality. The blue wall of silence you formed to protect a fellow officer. It was how Roddick ended up getting suspended and eventually quitting the force.

When Roddick's chief of police was arrested and charged with stealing money from a stripper, it shined an ugly light on the corruption and persistent problems going on with the North Providence police. The Department already had a volatile relationship with the mayor, so not even hours after the chief was charged, the mayor told the media he was "going to clean up the department".

This meant Roddick, along with many of his fellow officers, were put on immediate suspension pending further review. Roddick knew he was done as a cop. He was tangled up in too much shadiness. Two of his good friends who were also out on suspension, Toney Bruzzone and Shaun Higgens, had lined up replacement jobs doing well-paying executive protection gigs at the MGM Grand. Roddick went along with them to Vegas when they flew in for the interviews. He ended up never leaving.

The town just seemed to fit where he was at in his life. New beginnings. So he flew back, packed up his belongings into the old Toyota he had at the time and headed to the desert. He had taken the tourist advertisement of coming to Vegas and leaving his troubles behind literally.

Roddick got on the police's radar shortly after being licensed by the Nevada State Private Investigators Licensing Board (NSPILB). He was able to get friendly with a few of them on some of his early insurance fraud cases, one which involved a transient squatter getting burned alive in a foreclosed house that was intentionally set on fire.

The detectives and officers he had contact with knew he was a former cop and like most good cops, ran a background on him. They knew the particulars of his situation. That only made them even chummier with him. The way they saw it, he was a fellow officer getting screwed over by the system and politics. They knew the same could happen to them at any moment.

So he let them think he was a victim of the system. It was always wise to be on very good terms with local law enforcement if you ever wanted to have any real success in the private sector of investigation.

Shortly after making the call to the police, Roddick was pleased to see a familiar face in detective Jeffrey Chase from the LVMPD homicide department answering the call.

Chase was a clean cut local. Played quarterback for the Cheyenne High School varsity team. He was even being looked at by college scouts until he crashed his motorcycle shortly after his senior year homecoming game. He only ended up with a few cracked ribs, but it was enough to scare the scouts into thinking he was too reckless.

The moment he mentioned all this in their casual introduction, Roddick knew he had an in. All it took was a few beers at the bar and letting Chase go on about his high school glory days and possibly being a college star, and Roddick had him. From that point on, Chase would freely and without hesitation tell Roddick whatever he wanted to know about an ongoing investigation.

The apartment was now crowded with cops and a medicolegal along with a forensic pathologist from the Clark County Coroner/Medical Examiner's Office. They didn't have to do much examination to get an idea of cause of death. The hole in his head was a dead giveaway. One of them was going through the dead man's wallet to determine positive identification and start the process of finding next of kin.

"What have you got yourself into this time," Chase said, as he pulled Roddick aside.

Roddick laughed. "You know us New Englanders, always having to kick the fucking hornet's nest around if shit gets too quiet."

"Working a case?" Chase asked.

Roddick nodded. "Simple locate job."

"Suppose no point in asking for whom?"

Roddick smiled. "Wish I could. Wouldn't get much return business if I was known to spill to the cops every time they asked. And yes, I'm fully aware I have no privilege to do so."

"That rules out you working for a lawyer on this one."

"Always the clever one."

"We'll figure it out soon enough. You might as well tell me now instead of having to bring you in for further questions."

The room was getting more crowded with forensics grabbing every piece they deemed relevant and dropping them into plastic baggies with chain-of-custody/evidence labels on them.

Being the sharp detective he was, Chase could tell what Roddick was thinking and jerked his head toward the door. "Getting stuffy in here, let's go outside."

The air was cool as the temperature at this time of year dropped dramatically after sundown. It would be a few more months before you wouldn't be able to escape the heat, even at night.

Flashing lights of police cars blocking the entrance lit the parking lot up as residents stood outside either being interviewed by police as possible witnesses or just trying to see what was going on.

"Landlord said Rivera's only been here a few months. Paid everything in cash, including first and last month's rent."

These days someone paying in nothing but cash would have drawn suspicion. There were few places you could rent without putting down some form of plastic. But this was Vegas.

"That Glock left behind didn't have any serial numbers, did it?" Roddick asked.

Chase shook his head. "Nope. Didn't expect it would."

Roddick had seen his share of ghost guns as a cop. They were becoming more and more common to get online. That was because you could sell a gun frame eighty percent made completely legal without a background check. The remaining twenty percent wasn't difficult to do even for an amateur. Just some minor drill work.

"It's a 3:1 shot forensics isn't going to turn up shit," Roddick said. "Nor are you going to find any witnesses. This was a professional job."

"Looks like it," Chase said. The lackadaisical attitude Chase had came from a place of seeing every type of craziness imaginable to where there were no surprises left. Roddick knew the feeling well.

"I'll get a hold of my client, see if they'd be willing to divulge any more information that might help your investigation."

"That'd be most helpful," Chase said. "You know how to reach me."

Chase went back inside as Roddick continued staring off at the Luxar Sky Beam. The thing was so bright the FAA approved it as an aviation landmark as it could be seen at flight level as far as Los Angeles. To Roddick, it was nothing but a beacon attracting all the human insects in so they could get a good zapping.

Chapter 5

"You look distracted," Kaylee said, over bites of her sandwich. She had met Roddick for lunch between classes at the sandwich shop they both liked near Vegas' oldest dive bar Dino's Lounge. A place where Roddick was elected by the bartenders the prestigious title of "Drunk of the Month" for the first month he arrived in the city.

"Sorry. Just an unproductive morning trying to locate a guy."

Roddick had wasted all morning trying to get a hold of Lockhart. When that failed, he attempted to find more information on Rivera but came up with nothing useful.

"You should tell me who it is," she said. "I'm good at doxing people."

Roddick shook his head and swallowed a bite of his melt. "I know you are. But this cat was murdered by a professional, and I'm not about to get you involved in that."

Her large green eyes widened. "Too late. This sounds interesting as fuck."

"Christ, you kiss your mother with that mouth?"

Kaylee dropped the remainder of her sandwich on to the tray. "Had to spoil a nice lunch by bringing her up."

"You know, one of these days you're going to have

to tell me what is it between you two."

"It's simple. She doesn't get me, and she never has."

Roddick was going to pry further but was distracted when she pulled a 16-ounce energy drink out of her backpack and cracked it open.

"How many of them heart attacks in a can are you drinking now?"

She shrugged. "Depends. One or two. Three during finals. It's fine. If I get too jacked up I just end up taking Valium. How I made it through high school."

"I'm sure your mother approved of this."

"Stop bringing her up. And no, she didn't. But she was too busy being a big shot female lawyer to really give a fuck. All she cared about is if I got good grades so she could brag about it to her jerkoff lawyer friends."

"I'm sure she wasn't that bad."

"No, she was worse. She had my entire life planned out. I'd be going to the same college as her, and then when I passed the bar, we'd become this bullshit mother-daughter law firm."

Roddick couldn't help but laugh. "What can I say, sometimes parents have unrealistic expectations. My old man wanted me to be a doctor."

It was Kaylee's turn to laugh. "Yeah, right. You a doctor? What was he thinking?"

"Finish your sandwich, smartass."

****

The setting sun cast a burning orange hue over the valley. The Scorpion knew he'd only have a few more minutes of shooting left. He was out in the desert seven miles south of M Resort off South Las Vegas Boulevard. It was a common place for plinking, and you could tell. The ground was a blanket of spent shotgun shells, shot up junk, and broken glass bottles. He blended right in with the other shooters firing around him.

The supplier he got his guns from also threw in some targets and Tannerite. He first fired the Glocks he had assembled to make sure there weren't any problems with them. From there, he did drills for different types of reloading, ranging from emergency, speed, and tactical reloads.

Next, he tried the shotgun. He had sawed the barrel below eighteen inches approved by the ATF, along with stock which made the overall gun below the legal twenty-six inches. He fired 00 Buckshot at rusted tin cans and beer bottles at close range, making sure to choke up.

He closed the day with a custom AR-15 with a drop-in trigger so he could switch from semi to nearly fully automatic. For a target, he found a shot up refrigerator that a band of coyotes were foraging and stocked it full of the three pounds of Tannerite.

The first few shots he hit the fridge on semi-auto with no effect. He switched over to fully auto and unloaded into the center of it. The fridge erupted in flames as the door ripped off, and hit the dirt and went edgewise toward the Scorpion. He shifted to the side, but the door hit the ground again causing it to bounce up like a rocket before falling only a few feet from him.

The spectacle was enough to cause the shooters around him to stop and watch in a mixture of horror and amazement. The fridge was fully engulfed as the flammable insulation fueled the flames.

"Goddamn!" someone yelled.

The Scorpion clenched his fist at the attention he'd brought. It was time to go.

Chapter 6

Roddick was back at the apartments on Cambridge by nine the next morning. He wanted to talk to the landlord. He pulled into the vacant spot in front of a sign that read Apartments for Rent with a red arrow that pointed to the manager's office.

The office was similar to his own. Secondhand desk and an uncomfortable chair. Some filing cabinets with half-dead plants on top of it. Behind the desk was the wind-dried landlady. She had wavy brown hair starting to gray but you could easily tell she was once an attractive woman. The miles she had put on since then along with an unforgiving Nevada sun had aged her well beyond her actual years.

She didn't even bother to stand up as Roddick introduced himself.

"I'm Joe Roddick. I'm a private investigator. I was wondering if you could fill—"

"I already wasted all last night talking to the police. I got nothin' more to say. Especially to no private investigator."

Roddick grinned. " 'Course not." He pulled out the chair in front of her and took a seat.

"I always look into businesses I'm going to visit. Habit I suppose. I gotta say, your apartments got some of the worst ratings I've seen in this town, and that's saying something."

The woman scuffed. "All lies."

"One former tenant wrote a review that said he found a camera in his shower. Another said he found you going through his apartment. A lot of folks saying this place is the worst apartments they've ever been to."

"I can't stop people from writing lies after I evict them for not paying their rent or following the guidelines."

"I understand," Roddick said. "Suppose I could get rid of these *lies* for you. I'm sure that'll help you fill in some of these vacancies."

From the small number of neighbors Roddick had seen last night, he was pretty sure most of the rooms were empty. That could only mean she had to be losing money from all the bad word of mouth.

The hostility drained from her voice. "You can do that?"

"Oh, yeah. Wouldn't be a problem at all."

She thought about it for a moment. "I don't know exactly what you want to know. But I'll tell you what I forgot to tell them cops. That Rivera boy that was murdered last night. When he first rented the place a few months back, someone else was with him. He called him Dice."

"How did you forget to tell a detail like that to the cops?"

She shrugged. "Must've slipped my mind. I don't like cops much."

"What'd this Dice look like?"

"Tall, sickly, skinny. Tweaker for sure. Meth head most likely. Scabs all over his face with one of them meth mouths. Hardly no teeth. I'm sure he's probably dead by now or close to it."

"Ever see him around here again?"

She shook her head. "Nope. Like I said. He's dead somewhere with a needle sticking out of him."

Roddick thanked her and took a generic business card she had stacked on the desk in case he had any follow-up questions.

He climbed back in his car and sat for a moment thinking of how he could find Dice. If he was a meth addict, he needed another user who hung around addicts, and he knew just the guy.

****

The Flamingo Casino was the oldest operating casino/hotel on the Strip. It was the casino that defined Vegas. From its gangster background of Bugsy Siegel to the tropical Miami/South Beach look and its famous glowing pylon of orange and pink plumes fanned out over the entrance.

Roddick rarely visited the Strip since becoming a resident, outside of work. Most locals didn't. You don't last long in Vegas if you did. He parked his car at Bally's and took the elevated pedestrian bridge over East Flamingo Road. As he was crossing, the Fountains of Bellagio were dancing like showgirls to the Pink Panther theme before ending with a giant 45-foot water blast. It was one of many things in Vegas that Roddick never got tired of seeing.

Earlier he had called Evan Littleton, a drug and gambling addict contact. As a private investigator, just like a cop, you had to have informants. They came in all shapes and sizes. The most valuable were usually the undesirables.

He searched the casino game room which had over a thousand slot machines, past three card and Caribbean

Stud poker tables, and a row of one-armed bandit Keno machines until he found Littleton sitting in front of a nickel slot called Cash Coaster. He was dressed in a bleached stained t-shirt and ripped jeans. Roddick could tell he wasn't doing very well because he kept running his hands nervously through his greasy, dirty blond hair.

Littleton had spent his life living off the public dole between drug and gambling binges that ended either in jail, OD'ing, or being beaten up savagely for welching on bets.

"For a second," Roddick said as he stood behind him. "When you told me to meet you here, I was worried you'd actually have a job. Can't tell you how glad I am to see your ass parked in front of a cheap slot machine."

"Fuck you," he mumbled, as he kicked the stool he was sitting on out and started to walk away. Roddick followed.

"I need you to find a guy for me. Goes by Dice. Tall, skinny, meth head. Looks like he's got one foot in the grave."

Littleton stopped and scuffed. "Sure, I'll get right on that."

Roddick gave him a cold stare that meant he wasn't kidding around.

"It'll cost you."

"How much you in hock for this time?"

Littleton shrugged. "Couple grand."

"What you need to do is find yourself a pimp, which shouldn't be too hard in this town, and start selling yourself out to the homosexuals. That's where the money is. Or as they say in the porn industry, 'pay to be gay.' "

"You're an asshole."

Roddick laughed. "Take it easy. I'm just busting your balls. But, I'll tell you what I will do. You get me in touch with Dice, and I'll delete them text messages you sent me last month. You know, when you were strung out on whatever shit you were injecting yourself with at the time, and admitted to that unsolved hit and run death on Charleston Boulevard last year. The one where the police are pretty damn sure it's you but are waiting for that last bit of evidence to get a full conviction. With them tougher hit and run laws they got now, you could be looking at two to twenty years."

Littleton started shifting his eyes around the casino, avoiding eye contact, then bent his head. "Fine, whatever. I'll see what I can do."

He left but not without mumbling a few choice words that caught the attention of a young, attractive hostess.

"Everything all right?" she asked Roddick.

"Sure, just a sore loser."

"Is there any other kind?" She smirked and walked off.

No. There isn't. Roddick watched her walk away.

****

The Scorpion kept the car at a near crawl as he wheeled it through the interlocking neighborhood streets. He wasn't driving the Challenger but a much fancier piece of British engineering. His mirthless face glowed an inhumanly greenish-blue from the lights of the vehicle's electronic interface. The whites of his eyes scanned back and forth, looking for something.

A raccoon strutted into his path but the Scorpion

made no effort to alter his course. The coon nibbled on a scrap of food he had dug out of someone's trash, not worried at the coming headlights. He'd grown accustomed to people swerving out of his way. The Scorpion rolled over him with his front tire, causing a slight bump in the car, and a thud from the trunk.

He was far enough on the outskirts of the city that most streets were empty. He hadn't passed another car since he pulled off the main road. There was nothing but rows of houses that all looked the same with the exception of a few poorly maintained ones. One of them had a stripped down Buick on blocks in the driveway and a dust-covered boat that had probably never been set in water in its entire miserable existence.

He kept going until he reached wrought iron gates that blocked him from driving into the back nine of a public golf course. He made a sharp turn and a right onto the next street and pulled the wheels parallel to the sidewalk. He killed the engine when the headlights from a lifted diesel truck shined its LEDs at him like a search light. He slid down in the seat and reached for his gun, tempted to shoot the lights out. He clenched the Glock's grip tight as the truck drove by, leaving a peacock tail of exhaust smoke that reeked of kerosene.

The Scorpion got out, locked the door behind him and casually started walking up the sidewalk. A few houses down, he tossed the keys into a metal trash can stuffed with torn out carpet and debris from a remodel job.

He kept walking in a slow, confident stride. Moving as if he were in a brigade of one.

Chapter 7

Less than fifteen minutes after he texted her, Kaylee was at Roddick's place. She was dressed in her normal outfit; T-shirt, flannel, jeans, an assortment of bracelets on both wrists, and a black tattoo choker. The Cowardly Lion mane she had as a kid was now straight and went down to her shoulders.

"What do you need my help with?" she asked. Roddick had never asked her for help on a case before, so it was hard for her to control her excitement.

"Yeah, nothing big," he said, as he led her to the dining room table. "I was wondering if maybe you could take down some bad reviews for this apartment. I told the landlady I would after she gave me some good information."

Roddick could see the disappointment come over her. "That's it? I thought it would be something more…exciting."

Roddick grinned. "Baby steps. Can you do it?"

"Sure," she grunted out, as she started to take her laptop out. "Easy-peasy."

"That's the stuff," he said.

The doorbell rang. It was Toney Bruzzone. A fellow Bruins fan and all-round sports fan, Roddick had invited him to watch the Bruins-Flyers game. The disadvantage of having an East Coast time on the West Coast was most home games were during working hours. But that was the beauty of DVRs.

Bruzzone had a stout build and well-defined jawline, giving him that cop look. To his annoyance, he would regularly get asked if he was a cop. Roddick suggested he grow his hair out and get a goatee.

He brought his usual 12-pack of cheap domestic beer, handing one to Roddick, as they parked in front of the flat screen.

The Bruins scored early off a wrist shot on a power-play. The Flyers answered back in the closing minutes to tie it up.

"Ever miss being a cop?" Toney asked during the intermission.

The question surprised Roddick. Not once since they'd moved to Vegas did they talk about their past lives.

"Fuck, no. I should've gone into the private sector a long time ago. Better money and don't got a bunch of superiors swinging their dicks around screwing everything up."

"Ain't that the truth? The money I'm making from doing this high-end security shit is insane. Making over a grand a week just escorting some pop singer from her suite to the Garden Arena. You should see this broad; she's batshit crazy. Every time I go to escort her she's either half naked or strung out on amphetamines."

"Nice."

"Still," Toney continued. "Don't mean I ain't pissed on how things went down."

Roddick set his empty beer bottle down and leaned forward on the coach.

"Got to let it go, man. What's done is done. Besides, last I heard, Providence is going to hell. Can't maintain law and order with a bunch of boy scouts."

"Fuck that town," Toney cheered as he popped the cap to his fourth beer.

****

The Scorpion found an older diner with a boomerang-shaped roof and slid into one of the empty booths. The middle-aged waitress was quick to pour him coffee that tasted like she emptied the ashtrays into it. The food was better. He ordered a medium-rare 13-ounce T-bone with steak fries as a side.

Between bites, he observed the few customers in the place. One fat man sat at the counter. The rolls on the back of his bald head looked like a stack of pancakes. Two booths from him a homely woman with a four-finger forehead chatted it up with some disinterested middle-aged man. He nodded as she kept going while looking down to the right of him. Most likely his phone. He figured if he pretended to look interested long enough she would stop talking and he could take her to some cheap motel or the back of his car.

The waitress refilled the Scorpion's cup with the same awful coffee, but he drank it anyway. He was almost done with his steak when a tall blonde, who had ordered a cherry pie, moved toward him. She had an average face, but her body made up for it. Full breasts, long legs, and a high, sculpted ass that showed she didn't skip yoga class.

"Sorry, I ain't looking for a good time," he told her.

Her mouth slightly opened. "Excuse me? I'm not a whore!"

The Scorpion shrugged and took a sip of his coffee,

fighting to keep it down. "Then what do you want?"

"You looked like you could use the company."

"Do I now?"

"Yes, you do."

He wasn't surprised at her boldness. Women, for whatever reason, were drawn to him as if he stirred dormant primitive desires in them. She was no exception as she took a seat across from him, setting the pie box beside her.

"You going to eat all that tonight?" he asked.

"Oh, no. It's not all for me. It's for a lunch at the salon I work at on Sahara. I promised to bring a dessert."

He nodded, hoping it would spare him from the details of her life as a hairdresser. He wasn't so fortunate.

"I've done a lot of big name celebrities' hair."

'Course she had.

"Like Mariah Carey when she was at Caesars Palace."

This elicited no reaction from him as he cut the remainder of his steak. His indifference seemed to discourage her but only temporarily. After the briefest moment of silence, she tried to turn the tables on him.

"You here for business or pleasure?"

"Business," he said, pushing his plate aside.

"A conference I take it."

"That's right."

"For what?"

The Scorpion had made sure to look into conferences going on in case he was asked. "Marketing and branding. Nothing exciting."

"Have you done any ad campaigns I might have

seen?"

"Probably," he said, refusing to elaborate.

There was another brief silence.

"I'm Audrey, by the way."

She extended a well-manicured hand which he let awkwardly hang in the air before he finally shook it.

"Rick."

"Like the Pawn Star guy."

"Yeah, like the Pawn Star guy."

She smiled and slid out of the booth.

"Listen, Rick, I probably should be going. I don't live that far if you want to come for a drink. You do drink?"

"Occasionally."

"Well, I promise you, it'll be better than what you're drinking now. The coffee here is terrible.

"Yes, it is."

****

She was right; she didn't live that far from the diner. It was a small, one-bedroom affair with modest furnishings. She poured them both some bourbon and they sat on her second-hand sofa. He let her do most of the talking as he nursed his drink. Things progressed from there and ended with him dominating her, mostly from behind, which she seemed to enjoy.

When it was over, she lay beside him, a sweaty, panting mess. Sleep came over her fast, but he waited a good while to make sure she wouldn't be waking up. He quietly dressed and left her sleeping as he let himself out, but not before leaving a few $20s on her kitchen counter.

Chapter 8

The coffee tasted good as Roddick sat slightly hungover at the donut shop next to his office. He hadn't planned on drinking so much, but that's what usually happened when Toney came over. They'd finished the beer he brought and moved on to raiding the liquor cabinet and ended the evening with him passed out on the couch.

He didn't remember Kaylee leaving but was sure she was probably annoyed. She didn't like it when he drank so much. Most women didn't. After he woke, showered, and downed a dozen or so aspirin, he went straight to the Lucky Hearts Casino. He wanted to know where Lockhart was but nobody at the casino was much help.

"He ain't here," Frank Valentas, the casino's security director told him.

"Do you know where he might be?"

"What do I look like, his girlfriend? How the hell should I know?"

With nothing else to do, it was a day at the office doing routine background checks that companies outsourced to him and paperwork for the claims adjusters. He hoped to hear from Littleton soon or else this case was dead in the water.

****

The Scorpion punched in the code he was given

into the key variable loader and waited for it to send the signal to the dash scanner he had bought. A few seconds later he could hear the police radio chatter. It had taken longer than he wanted to get a working scanner due to the Vegas police switching to cryptic channels. The media still had access, and that was how his supplier was able to get a working code. Some guy who owed a lot in gambling debt and who worked at a small-time community paper had supplied the necessary digits.

He listened in as patrol officers communicated with dispatch while checking the time. He had one more job to do and then he only needed to wait until the rest of his payment was transferred, and that would be it.

Perhaps he'd stick around and do some gambling. Why not? He could afford to be a little reckless with his money. He had enough dough locked away that he could quit now and live comfortably. But doing what exactly? Guys like him didn't settle down, raise families, and spend their remaining days getting fat and playing golf.

He started the engine and listened as it growled awake before smoothing out. He enjoyed the sound of a well-engineered machine. He never had the radio playing when he drove. He wanted to hear the engine and the sounds it gave off.

He punched the accelerator as he pulled out and the engine roared down the road. He got it up to 90 before he backed off and let it cruise back down to the posted speed limit. A few miles down he passed a parked cruiser doing speed checks. He didn't even look twice as he drove by.

****

Littleton texted Roddick when he was on his way home. The text simply read *trailer park on Mojave*.

Roddick did a U-turn on Las Vegas Boulevard and a right on east Sunset Road. A few turns later he jumped onto I-515 going north. He had an idea of which trailer park Littleton had texted about. It would be an ideal place to cook meth. Most of the inhabitants there did.

He could see the smoke once he got onto Mojave. The park looked like a firefighters convention. Company engines and first responders filled the small roadway between small, crumbling singlewide mobile homes, derelict RVs with busted out windows, and tireless motorhomes with garlands of trash and waste around them.

Not able to get around the engines, Roddick pulled his car to the side, parked, got out and walked to where the action was. He followed two lines of crossed hoses to where they were shooting high-pressure streams at one of the model homes burning. It had all the outward appearance of a meth lab explosion.

This was confirmed when one of the fire crew told Roddick to get back; the fumes were toxic. Several paramedics were already treating fire fighters who had directly inhaled the smoke when they tried to make their way inside the home.

Roddick made a call to Detective Chase, letting him know he should probably come by. While he waited, he watched as rescuers pulled a badly charred body out before the structure caved in on itself.

Chase arrived in a white Nissan Maxima. Though it was an unmarked police car, it might as well have been. The over-tinted windows and lack of hubcaps made it pretty easy to tell it belonged to the department. That's why Roddick never bothered with unmarked police cars. He just rolled around North Providence in his comfortable Interceptor Utility.

"Glad you could make it to the cook-out," Roddick said. "They pulled out a crispy one 'bout ten minutes ago."

Chase glanced at what was left of the mobile home. The fire crew had put most of the fire out. Only a smoldering skeleton structure remained.

"It was bound to happen," Chase said. "This whole place is full of meth-mobiles. Can't do much about it. Shut a few down and ten more crop up. It's all about containment, if you know what I mean."

Roddick knew exactly what he meant. Keep the trash out of the nice parts of town, away from tourists and casinos, the life blood of the city.

"You going to tell me how you think this is related to the Rivera murder?"

"I'm pretty sure that body they pulled out is a man named Dice. He was pals with Rivera."

"How do you know?"

"I got my sources," Roddick said.

Chase scowled but knew not to push it further.

The media had shown up and officers moved in and pushed them back.

"You don't think this is simply a case of some amateur cook blowing himself up?"

Roddick shook his head.

"It would be mighty coincidental, him doing that just as I was coming to question him. I think this was the work of the same professional that killed Rivera."

"Possibly. We'll have to see what the coroner's

office has to say as the cause of death. But if you are right, that means this is some serious shit, and I'm going need to know who you are working for."

Under normal circumstances, Roddick would have no problem going to jail to protect the confidentiality of his client. But since he was unable to get in touch with Lockhart, perhaps he could use police efforts in tracking him down.

"Jay Lockhart."

"Jay Lockhart, who runs the Lucky Heart Casino?"

"That's right?"

"Why did he want you to find Rivera?

Roddick shrugged. "Didn't really go into specifics. I'd done simple locate jobs for him before. He usually did it for his loan shark pals."

"When was the last time you spoke with him?"

"I haven't spoken with him since he asked me to do the job. I went by the casino earlier, but they weren't very forthcoming."

Chase laughed. "They never are. Okay, I'll put a BOLO out for him. I need to talk to him."

"You and me both," Roddick agreed.

Chapter 9

The Scorpion went back to the same boomerang-roofed diner as the night before and ordered a jalapeno cheeseburger and a beer from a butch-haired waitress whose barber must've been the front end of a lawnmower.

From one of his many burner phones, he got onto the diner's Wi-Fi to scroll through various news sites as he waited. The trailer park fire was the top story locally. He shook his head. The job went down smoothly. When he'd gotten the address of his next target and was told he was probably cooking meth, The Scorpion didn't want to take any chances inhaling that shit. He'd picked up a disposable chemical suit from a hardware store along with an industrial respirator mask.

He pulled right up to the trailer, rapped on the door, and when his mark opened it, naked from waist up with a lit cigarette dangling from his mouth, he stuck the sawed-off into his chest and let him have it. He was dead before he hit the floor, landing like so many of them do with his ankles crossed. The shot echoed louder than he wanted, so he didn't stick around. If he had, he would've found where the cigarette landed.

Even someone unfamiliar with the process of cooking meth knew the risk of an explosion at any time was high. Yet, this amateur was making the shit while carelessly smoking away. Left to his own devices, the

Scorpion knew it was only matter of time before his target without his doing would've blown himself straight to hell. He just sped it along for him.

He sipped his beer and found it to be worse than the coffee. It was warm and flat with an aftertaste similar to the bathwater of a skunk. Thankfully, the food came, and it was just what he needed. The added heat to the burger made the greasy pattie pop. He knew it was a good burger by the dribble of fat that fell onto his plate. He washed it down with the beer and felt a sense of satisfaction until Audrey came in and went straight to where he was seated.

"I told you, I'm not a whore," she said, dropping the twenties he had left her on the table.

The Scorpion shrugged and said nothing. She shook her head.

"You're an ass."

She walked out as he picked the money up and started putting them back in his wallet. That's when he noticed the number on one of the twenties that wasn't there when he left it.

The butch-haired waitress came by to take his plate.

"Pretty girl."

"Yeah?" The Scorpion said, as he held up the twenty with the digits on it between his fingers. "You want her number?"

****

The phone rang as Roddick was pouring his second cup of coffee on the patio. It was Detective Chase.

"Got a call early this morning from someone in Centennial Hills, a neighbor presumably, complaining about the smell coming from a parked Jaguar XJ. The responding officer ran the plates and I think you can see where I'm going here."

"I'm on my way."

Roddick got the address from Chase and wasted no time heading out. The Centennial Hills were in the northwest area of the valley. It was an elevated location and great for people that wanted to live away from the casinos.

Lockhart's car was parked in one of the neighborhood areas of Prairie Meadows Street and Western Saddle Avenue. Chase's Nissan Maxima was surrounded by several police cars. Roddick could smell it before he even opened the door. The recognizable odor of something dead.

He stepped out and greeted Detective Chase as one of the officers worked a slim-jim on the driver's side window.

"Someone just now reported the smell?" Roddick asked.

"It never ceases to amaze me what people will put up with to not get involved."

The officer got the door open and popped the trunk. That's when the full force of the odor came. It was strong enough to cause one of the nearby officers to start dry heaving. Roddick covered his mouth with his shirt.

"Christ," Chase yelled as he shielded his nose with the crook of his elbow and they both stepped closer to get a look inside.

A bloated mound of flesh greeted them. It was hard to tell what it was at first. Though the grotesque, bloated face looked more like the Elephant Man, Roddick knew it was Lockhart. His eyes hadn't changed.

"Is it him?" Chase asked, his voice muffled as he kept his nose covered.

Roddick nodded and kept looking until the smell and sight of it all was too much. He turned and went toward his car. Chase followed.

"This is getting out of hand," Chase said.

Roddick stopped and turned toward him. "We got to get out in front of this guy, or we're just going to keep picking up after him."

"How do you figure we do that?"

"I got a plan."

"Which is?"

Roddick didn't answer as he got in his car and backed out. Chase didn't go after him. He knew it was probably best if he didn't know.

Chapter 10

Roddick sent an annoyed kid working the gaming floor to fetch Valentas. As he waited, he watched some cocky out-of-towner get taken down a few notches at the craps table. After losing big the previous game, he kept at it, rolling a six on the come out roll. He rolled a few more times, unable to match the point and sevened out as the kid came back and signaled for Roddick to follow. Not even an hour in Vegas and he probably already wanted to leave as the two standing dealers collected his losing bet and paid off the side bets.

Roddick followed the kid to the back hallway and into the same room full of security monitors. This time instead of Lockhart sitting behind the monitors it was Valentas. Roddick, until recently, had only brief interactions with the stocky, slicked-back black-haired man. At the time, he had taken his orders from Lockhart, but now, just as Roddick had figured, he was calling the shots.

"If you're here to tell me about what happened to Jay, I already know."

Roddick took the seat across from him. "I'm sure you do. Nothing gets past you casino boys."

Valentas frowned. "Why are you here?"

"I knew you'd be the one moving into Jay's spot, so I figured I might as well fill you in on what I was doing for Jay."

"I know what you were doing, and your services will no longer be required."

Roddick tried to look disappointed. "That's too bad. See, Jay told me everything. And I mean everything."

"Did he now?"

"Yup. I know all about Rivera and why he was killed. He told me because he was sure he was going to get killed himself. Turns out, he was right."

"Why was Jay killed?"

Roddick stood up.

"Why should I tell you? My services are no longer needed, right?"

"That's your angle, is it? You think holding this over me is going to get you some work?"

"Maybe."

Valentas laughed. "Jesus, business that bad for you, is it? Think you can try and blackmail me into giving you handouts like one of them Elvis-wannabe panhandlers outside?"

"Sure. You look dumb enough to go for it."

"Get out and don't ever come back. You ain't welcomed at this casino no more."

In the old mafia-ran Vegas days, a threat of leg breaking would have been made at this point. Times were different, but the threat remained. It was just unspoken. He knew as soon as he walked out he had just put himself in the crosshairs of a very dangerous man. And he wasn't talking about Valentas.

****

The Scorpion didn't expect to be getting another job on what he planned to be his final day in the city. So much for gambling. He was sitting across the street from a donut shop. The only listing his new target had was in a small office next to it. The lot was empty except for cars pulling in and out of the donut shop.

It was almost noon when a white Nissan Altima drove in and parked in front of the office. The man that got out fit the description he was given, right down to stubble on his face. He usually didn't care what their backgrounds were except when they were similar to this guy's. A former cop now working as a private investigator meant no mistakes could be made. It'd been a long time since he'd had to take down a formidable target.

"361, insurance confirmed, Dodge Ram, no warrants, no locals," a female officer blurted over the scanner. "That's clear."

He turned the volume down and watched as cars sped down Las Vegas Boulevard at high speed. He counted four possible wrecks that nearly happened in the span of fifteen minutes. The worst being a fat man on a motorcycle coming close to being run over by a limousine. The bike put out a guttural sound that brand of road bike was known for as he revved the throttle high and narrowly missed the front end of the limousine as he cut through lanes.

Shortly past noon his target came out of his office and went into the donut shop. The Scorpion moved in while his back was toward the window. He crossed the busy street and closed in on the Altima. He reached underneath the car and placed a small magnetic GPS tracker on the metal frame.

The man came out with an ample size coffee cup and glazed donut dangling from his mouth as the Scorpion crawled back to the Challenger. From his phone, he entered the tracker code into a website and waited for the satellite to hone in. The Scorpion had used similar devices before but preferred this one for its more accurate real-time tracking. Once it had locked on to the Altima, the Scorpion started the engine and pulled out.

He was finishing a late lunch at a nearby sandwich shop when he got the notification that the car was moving. Back on Las Vegas Boulevard, he kept his distance. Most people on the road were in their private bubble when driving. Oblivious to those around them and especially who was behind them. But not this guy. He would know if someone was following him. It was why the Scorpion chose to use the tracking. No mistakes.

The Altima kept a steady speed of 45 mph before making a right on Tropicana for a mile and then another right before making a stop. As he closed in, the Scorpion could see the car had turned into a grocery store. Next to the store was a fast food joint. The Scorpion pulled into that parking lot and killed the engine. *Hopefully, his next stop is home.*

****

The whole drive from his office, Roddick had the feeling he was being followed. He kept checking the mirrors but saw nothing. No recognizable cars. Every vehicle he thought may have been the one following turned off.

He needed to get some things at the store, and it would be a good time to assess the situation. He pulled into the store parking lot and drove in to the first open spot. There he waited several minutes to see if any familiar vehicles pulled in. Nothing. Rubbing his head for a moment, he got out. He needed a drink. Later.

In the store, he walked past a row of people playing slots. These people had to be the most degenerate gamblers of them all. You had to be if you couldn't even make it through getting eggs and butter without having to hit up the slots.

He grabbed a few pieces of fried chicken and potato wedges from the deli and a case of bottled water. The feeling of being watched remained as he got back in his car. *Tracking device? Possibly.*

But if he were being tracked, he would not be able to search the vehicle for it without them noticing. Maybe he was paranoid? That was a possibility as well, but he had to trust his gut. He would proceed according to plan. He started the engine and pulled out.

****

He stayed on Tropicana before merging onto 1-515 north. From there, he kept his distance on the highway. Traffic was picking up. It seemed every type of bad driver was converged on the road. The Scorpion was currently stuck behind a minivan full of kids with California plate, driving well below the speed limit. To his right, a billboard truck that read Hot Totally Naked Ladies at Big Daddy's. He could see several of the kids' faces pressed against the window trying to read the sign. The Scorpion smirked.

He stayed on the interstate for several more miles before the car turned off on West Lake Mead and then into the driveway of a two-story stucco house. The Scorpion didn't even bother slowing down. Instead, he drove straight past. He would be back.

Chapter 11

Earlier in the day before going to the office, Roddick had stopped at the house on West Lake Mead. It was currently abandoned like so many homes in the Las Vegas Valley since the recession hit. This brought in an influx of squatters. Many of the foreclosed houses were ransacked and became places for criminal activity to go down.

Roddick was brought in by a bank who owned the leases to several foreclosed homes in the area to photograph the damage and to kick out squatters. They had broken the front door locks several times, to where it was pointless to replace them until now. He needed this particular place to look like someone was living there. So he slapped on a new front lock, hung some curtains to cover the windows, and brought in battery-powered lights.

The sun was starting to set now as he pulled in. He hurried to grab his food and bottled water and took them inside. He turned on the battery-powered lamps and placed them around the house to light it up.

The backyard was secured by a masonry block wall that was common with Las Vegas properties to cut out the noise and add privacy from the busy streets many homes bordered on. It was a nice set-up except for the empty pool filled with trash, needles, and broken bottles.

"Parasites," Roddick said out loud. "The whole lot of them."

He went back inside and retrieved a KSG-25 bullpup shotgun he had left earlier. Because both of the dual tubes held 12 rounds including one in the chamber, Roddick spent several minutes loading the gun with an entire box of shotgun shells.

With the gun full, he took it along with the food and water up to the top level of the stairs so he had an elevated view of the front door and area around the front of the house.

He had done stakeouts before but never ones where he was the bait. This made the waiting even more excruciating. He wasn't even sure if he was being followed. This could all end up being an entire waste of an evening.

The greasy food helped settle him down but only momentarily. As the hours crept by the doubt grew.

What if this hitman didn't show up? Figured out it really wasn't Roddick's place. Where would he strike instead? The private detective's real house when Kaylee was there? Roddick clenched the gun tight. *Just let him try.* The phone kept vibrating. Kaylee most likely. Or Detective Chase wanting to know what the hell he was doing. He wasn't even sure what he was doing at this point. What a stupid plan this was.

It was closing in on midnight when he couldn't take it anymore. His target wasn't coming. Discouraged, Roddick went down the stairs and was about to head out when he saw it. Movement from the back window. The son of bitch had breached the back wall! What the hell did he put himself up against? He tried to point the barrel toward the direction of the movement but was too late. A flashing blue flame scorched his eyes as he heard the sound of shattering glass and then nothing.

Chapter 12

It was the call she always dreaded getting. Though Kaylee hadn't seen her dad as much as she would have liked growing up, he had always been one of the most important parts of her life. She had never had the kind of bond with her mother as she did with him. And when she found out he was no longer a cop, the fear something might happen to him dissipated. How wrong she was.

She had just gone to sleep after spending all evening doing biology assignments she had put off. The call was from Sunset Hospital in Summerlin. All they would say was her dad had been recently admitted and she needed to come immediately. Fighting back tears, she quickly dressed and left.

The ER waiting room was empty except for an older woman waiting for her husband, who was having difficulty breathing. All the tired woman at the ER reception desk could tell Kaylee was that her dad arrived forty minutes ago. He had been shot and was currently being looked at by doctors.

As she waited for more news, she called Toney and Shaun. It didn't take both of them long to show up.

"Any news yet?" Shaun asked.

Shaun was a tall man, nearing 6'5", lean build, dark mustache showing bits of gray.

"Not yet," she said.

"I'm sure he's going to be fine, Kaylee," Toney said. "He's one tough son of a bitch."

Two police officers arrived and started asking the receptionist questions before the one in plain clothes came up to her.

"You must be Kaylee. I'm Detective Chase. Can I talk to you for a moment?"

Kaylee looked at Shaun then Toney, both seated and looking sternly at Chase.

"You can say whatever you have to say in front of them. They use to be cops with my dad."

Chase inspected them. Toney wasted no time giving a sly grin. "Yeah, what she said."

"Very well. Neighbors reported hearing a gunshot at a house on Lake Mead Boulevard. When the responding officers arrived, they found your dad unconscious. He had been shot once in the head. There was a shotgun nearby."

Kaylee's face turned white with the shock of it all. "What was he doing there?"

"We don't know exactly. You don't know about this house?"

She shook her head. "No, I don't."

Chase nodded.

"There's more you're not telling me."

"Yes, his wallet was missing. Might have been a robbery—"

She interrupted, "But you don't think it was."

"No."

"What was my dad involved in?"

Chase rubbed his chin and thought hard about what he was going to say next. "All I can say is your dad got himself possibly involved with some high profile murders by what might be a professional killer."

"A professional killer? You mean hitman?"

"Yes."

Toney and Shaun were on their feet now, standing behind Kaylee.

"Got any suspects on who this person might be?" Toney asked.

Chase shook his head. "Not at this time."

"He the same person that stuffed that guy from the Lucky Hearts Casino into the trunk of his own car?" Shaun asked.

"Possibly."

"Possibly." Toney snorted. "You Vegas boys couldn't find your asses with both hands and a flashlight."

"Sorry, we don't hold the same moral disregard as you New England cops," Chase snapped back.

"Just stop it, all of you," Kaylee said. "Is my dad going to be okay?"

"That's for the doctors to say," Chase replied.

"Boy, you've been a whole lot of helpful, haven't you," Shaun quipped.

Having had enough, she let them continue arguing as she searched for the closest soda machine. None of them carried energy drinks, so she just got a soda.

She was coming back down the hall when a stern-looking doctor came out asking for her.

"I'm Doctor Morrison," he said. "Your father sustained a perforating gunshot wound to the left side of his head. His vitals are currently stable, and it looks like the bullet didn't hit any major blood vessels, which is good. However, he got a moderate score on the Glasgow Coma Scale."

"Which means?"

"If it were any lower we normally wouldn't operate. We are going to do so to remove any gunshot debris. We will also be removing a portion of his skull to relieve the pressure. He will be in a medically-induced coma, but I have to tell you as of right now, the chances of survival are not looking very likely."

"I don't care. Do the surgery," Kaylee said, wiping tears from her eyes.

The doctor nodded and left. Shaun and Toney moved in closer. They had put their squabble with Detective Chase on hold to comfort her.

"He'll pull through," Shaun said.

Kaylee wasn't so sure now.

****

He watched the lights of commercial airlines landing and taking off at McCarran from a parked spot off Sunset Road. The Scorpion had heard over the scanner that Roddick was still alive but in critical condition and had been transported to Sunset Hospital. He turned the scanner off once he parked after seeing a sign on the chain link fence enclosing the airfield that read Tune your Radio to 10.1 FM to monitor Air Traffic Communications.

He listened to the air traffic for a while and then opened the wallet he had taken and took out Roddick's driver's license. His listed address was on the other side of town from where the Scorpion had followed him. The bastard knew he was coming and had tried to lay out a trap.

Had the Scorpion not taken extra precautions, like not going through the front door, it might have worked. The Scorpion felt validated in not underestimating

Roddick. Perhaps it was this respect he had given him that he didn't put an extra bullet in his head when he lifted his wallet to momentarily throw the cops off. That, or he was simply getting sloppy.

"LAS Tower: Delta 225, Las Vegas Tower, clear for take-off on runway 8L/26R... Copy Tower."

He watched as the 747 took off before starting the engine. It was time to leave this town.

Chapter 13

The surgery had gone as well as it could have. Kaylee's father was moved to an ICU room, where his vitals were watched by a steady flow of nurses. Kaylee stayed with him the entire night, but by morning one of the doctor's saw how exhausted she was and convinced her to go home and get some rest. They would contact her immediately if there was any change in his condition.

She didn't even remember the drive back to her dorm or crawling into bed still fully clothed. She slept into late afternoon until the reality of her situation woke her. Still groggy, she drove to the nearest convenience store and grabbed protein bars and several power drinks before going back to the hospital.

They had moved him out of the ICU and into a regular room. The doctor that checked up on him told her there was no change in his condition and nothing more they could do but wait.

She turned on the Vegas Golden Knights-Bruins game that they were supposed to go to on the TV for him. From the moment the puck dropped, the Golden Knights physically dominated the Bruins. Though the Bruins had more talent, it was a case of the whole not being the sum of its parts. The Golden Knights were more physical and hungry for the win.

By the third period, the Bruins were down by three

goals. In a play that was a perfect set-up for a shot on goal, the Bruins left wing froze after getting the puck, causing one of the Golden Knights defensemen to slam into him so hard he almost put both of them through the glass. This set off a scrum with several players, and once it was sorted out, the defenseman was sent to the penalty box, giving the Bruins a power play. Even Kaylee knew it was a bogus call. Not that it mattered, as the Bruins squandered the opportunity.

Each time they missed a goal shot, Kaylee found herself yelling at the ceiling-mounted television. She didn't realize how loud she was until one of the nurses opened the door and stuck her head in to make sure everything was okay.

Shaun and Toney came by during the final minutes and watched it with her, glancing at Roddick periodically to see if there was any response from him.

Kaylee's mom called several times during the day, but she let it go to voicemail. Now she was blowing up her phone with texts demanding to know how she was.

"I'm fine, Mom," she said as she stepped out into the hallway.

"Why haven't you returned my calls? I've been worried sick."

"About me or dad?"

"Both of you, of course."

She knew it was a lie but let it go.

"He's stable. There's nothing else that can be done but wait and hope he wakes up."

"Do you want me to come?"

Kaylee almost dropped her phone at the thought of her mother being there. "No! I'm fine. Dad's fine. There's nothing you could do being here."

There was a long pause before, "You know, I do care about your father. I never wanted him to end up like this. That's why I refused to put myself through being married to a cop."

But sleeping with one was okay.

"I know, Mom. I'll stay in touch, promise."

She felt bad when she hung up. She knew her mother cared about her well-being, she just couldn't deal with her right now.

****

The rest of the money had not been transferred yet. The Scorpion was not going to leave town until it did. Nor was he going to wait around either. He had only met his Vegas contact once.

He ran a pawn shop as a front on West Desert Inn Road. It was a small space located in a decrepit freestanding retail building with a souvenir shop next to it. Giant industrial air conditioners on top of the building that sounded like big block engines being revved up. A red hanging sign above the shop read Need Cash? Buy/Sell/Pawn

The Scorpion went in and found it to be a clutter of junk ranging from '50s style jukeboxes, signed sports memorabilia without any sort of proof of authentication, and a small glass display of rings, jewels, and coin pieces.

His contact was behind the wooden cash wrap. He had the look of a '70s porn director. Loud tropical shirt, half-buttoned exposing a thatch of black hamburger meat and a gold-colored disco medallion. This coupled with a bad comb-over on the top and frizzy sides that looked like superglued pubic hair.

"The rest of my payment hasn't gone through," the

Scorpion said as he stood in front of the counter.

"That's because you didn't do the job. That private investigator is still alive." He pointed up at the mounted television, which was showing the local news. Some young reporter was standing out front of the Summerlin Hospital.

"He's a vegetable. If he ever wakes up, I'll come back and take care of it."

"The hell you will."

The Scorpion saw the man's hand drop below the desk and promptly moved to the side as the bottom section exploded, sending splinters of wood and buckshot around where his crotch would have been. With his Glock already drawn, he put two slugs into the man's chest and watched him fall behind the counter.

Walking around to where he was laying, the Scorpion saw the double barrel the man had mounted under the counter with a set of magnets. He squatted down over him and watched as the ugly man gasped for air.

"You weren't ever going to pay me the rest of it, where you? Was your plan to finish me off from the start?"

"They don't want loose ends," the dying man gurgled as blood bubbled out his mouth.

"Who you working for?"

"Fuck you," he said and spat the blood in the Scorpion's face.

The Scorpion stood up, wiped the blood from his eyes, and emptied the remainder of the clip into the man's head. He went into the small bathroom in the back, washed the blood off the best he could, then broke down the office door and ripped out the DVR to the security cameras. He came back to the dead man and took out his wallet and phone. The phone was PIN protected, so he shut it off in case he had tracking on it. He'd try to get into it later.

He smashed the glass display case and pocketed some gold coins and jewelry to make it look like a robbery and left.

Chapter 14

It had been a busy morning for Detective Chase. When he got to the office, his voicemail was full of messages from the victim's family members and possible witnesses. It took a good part of two hours to go through them. Most of the witnesses confirmed what he already knew, and there was always a certain amount of abuse you took when telling people related to the deceased you had no new information for them.

Next, his sergeant had instructed him and Detective Kyle McCarthy to re-canvas the house on Lake Meade Avenue and go door-to-door around the neighborhood to see if anyone had seen anything.

The house had already been thoroughly processed by forensics when they got there. Chase stood near a small puddle of dried blood where Roddick had been shot and stared at the shattered sliding glass door that opened to the back patio. Ballistics confirmed from the ejected casing it was a Glock 9mm. The same kind used to kill Rivera and Lockhart.

The coroner report on Lockhart said he died from a gunshot wound to the back of the head. So, he was shot, stuffed in the trunk of his car, and driven to Centennial Hills and left.

They still hadn't been able to find the actual scene of the crime. Last known sighting of Lockhart was at a gas station on Tropicana where he'd filled up and bought a pack of cheap cigars.

"You still thinking this was all the same guy?" McCarthy asked, as if reading his mind.

Chase nodded. "I do."

Roddick had always liked McCarthy. He was new to the homicide unit but sharp as they came. Smarter than others who'd been working there for decades.

"What about that tweaker they pulled out of that burnt trailer? Coroner said he'd been shot at close range with a shotgun, not a 9mm?"

"I'm sure he has many different types of guns," Chase said. "Whatever best fits the job. Roddick was sure it was the same guy, and I trust his judgment. That, and I don't believe in coincidences. Him being friends with Rivera and having something like that happen to him shortly after Rivera was killed and before Roddick could talk to him. What are the chances?"

"I'd say slim. But why'd he take Roddick's wallet? He never took the others?"

"Can't say. He wants to shake things up. Create doubt. Make it look like a break-in burglary gone wrong, get us all pointed in the wrong direction long enough for him to slip through the cracks. But honestly, as of right now, that's my best guess.

"You find out why Roddick was here?"

"I got a hold of the bank that owns the property. They confirmed they hired Roddick to document the damage transients had caused and to check on the place periodically to make sure there were no more squatters."

"So, maybe he just walked in on something going down and…"

"I told you, our killer would like us to think that.

Roddick said he had a plan. I think he somehow got the killer's attention and lured him here."

"To do what? I heard stories of Roddick being a dirty cop in Providence. How do we know he isn't more involved in this?"

"If you actually studied up on him, you'd know he wasn't that kind of dirty cop. His intent was probably to take the dude out himself."

"Then he got what was coming to him."

Chase didn't respond.

With nothing fresh coming to them, they set out knocking on doors. The first woman was the one that made the 911 call. She was in her late sixties, with a swollen stomach, and short, gray hair.

"I've been calling you guys for months about the riffraff coming in and out of that place. It finally takes someone getting shot for you to show any interest. Just last month me and my husband are pulling in, and we see two of them bums standing out front of that place. Tell us they're our new neighbors. The hell they are, I say. Call the police, and you send one police car by only to tell us there ain't much they can do."

"He's correct, ma'am. I suggest you call the mayor's office," McCarthy said.

They didn't get much useful information from her as she was getting ready for bed when she heard the shots.

The next neighbor they spoke to, a jocular middle-aged man named Wayne Parson, said he was outside drinking and BBQing with some friends when he heard the shots and went to the front to see where they came from. He said he thought he saw a red BMW he hadn't seen before in the area earlier that evening. This was contradicted by another resident, an elderly man who was out walking his dog, who said it was a silver Lexus, not a BMW.

"A whole lot of nothing," Chase said as they got in the car.

"Somebody had to have seen something."

"Doesn't appear to be the case."

In all his years of being a detective, he hadn't seen anything like this. A trail of bodies and nothing to go on. He didn't like this situation at all.

Chapter 15

The first of several alarms she had set went off. It was for her morning chemistry class, but Kaylee had no intention of going. She'd spent most of the night at the hospital. Her father still hadn't shown any signs of waking up, and the nurses and doctors that would check in all had the same grave look. She knew it would be only a matter of time before they talked of pulling his feeding tube.

She got up, showered, and grabbed a bagel and energy drink before driving to her dad's house. She wanted to get some personal effects to put in his room. Maybe that would help rouse him. She'd heard that people in comas were aware of their environment and could listen to people talking to them. She didn't know how much of that was true. But it at least gave her a sense of trying to do something to help.

She half expected to find cops parked in the driveway when she pulled up. They had been hanging around the hospital, and Detective Chase would come by with more questions she couldn't answer.

"Did he say anything about his plans that night? We had our tech people look at his phone, but he deleted almost everything off it as if he was expecting it to be looked at. Did he do this often? Did he ever talk to you about the reasons he was put on suspension in Providence?"

Kaylee knew he was just doing his job and becoming frustrated as she was not coming up with answers. But the constant barrage of questions annoyed her to where she was trying to avoid him.

She used the spare key her dad had given her to let herself in. It was unsettling how quiet it was. Roddick always had some type of noise going on, just like herself. Whether it was music playing or the television. They never liked dead silence.

To remedy it, she slipped her earbuds on and listened to a playlist of techno-punk, dubstep, and electronic rock as she went to his room. She stuffed one of his Bruins jerseys in her backpack, along with a 5x7 framed picture from her senior year off his dresser. The photograph was of her sitting in front of the water fountain in DePasquale Square in Providence. Her mother had made her get her makeup done for the picture, which Kaylee hated. It was excessive and slutty for her taste.

So engrossed with her dislike of the picture she didn't notice him watching her from the doorway until she turned to leave. Normal girls would have screamed but having been around her dad enough she had grown accustomed to the unexpected.

He stood a little over six feet, with prominent, hollowed out cheekbones, and military-style short blond hair with a little product to spike it up. Kaylee couldn't lie, he was nice to look at except his eyes. They were the soulless eyes of the damned.

In his right hand was a gun. She knew enough about guns to know it was a Glock 9mm. The same kind the police told her Roddick was shot with.

"You're the one that shot my dad?"

The Scorpion didn't reply.

"Why are you here?"

He stepped toward her direction. Every inch of her being wanted to run but she held her ground. "I was looking for information on who your dad was working for."

"Why?"

He moved in closer.

"You're in danger but not from me. If I were you, I would find a place to lay low for a while."

He turned and left without making a sound. Kaylee blinked hard to make sure she wasn't hallucinating.

"What the fuck was that?"

****

Detective Chase kept looking at the profile he was given for his would-be hitman. He was looking for a white male, between 30-50 years old, average height, build, possible military background.

He dropped the paper on his desk and started rubbing his temples. "Fucking profilers," he grumbled. Completely useless but they needed to appease the media and family members when they had little else to give them.

McCarthy laughed and asked, "Should I put a bulletin out to be on the lookout for every white male under fifty years old?"

"Knock yourself out," Chase said as he leaned back in his chair. It was not a productive day as far as getting any new information. He was about to pack it in and start fresh in the morning when he got the call.

"Detective Chase… uh-huh… I'll be right there."

"What's up?" McCarthy asked.

"Night employee at that pawn shop on West Desert

Inn Road found the manager shot. Responding officer thinks it's a 9mm."

McCarthy shrugged. "Other people use that caliber too. Not just our guy."

"Still worth checking out, wouldn't you say?"

"Yeah, I suppose."

Chapter 16

He waited as she got into a blue Chevy Sonic and drove off. No rush. He had placed the same magnetic tracker he used on her dad underneath her car. No doubt her old man had taught her to be aware of her surroundings.

The Scorpion followed her GPS signal onto Highway 215 toward Henderson. He was getting used to maneuvering through the cluster of clueless drivers. She got off on exit 10 and headed toward Wayne Newton Boulevard. He had a good idea where she was going. They were closing in on the University.

He pulled on to South Maryland Parkway and followed her to the student parking off Tropicana. He parked and watched as she put her earbuds back in and started walking to the dorm buildings. She acknowledged a few students standing outside smoking, taking a few puffs from one of them before going inside.

The Scorpion killed the engine and waited. He wasn't sure what exactly for, but he knew the moment when she said her old man was the private detective he'd shot that she would be the one to lead him to the men he wanted.

The police chatter ate up some time until he grew weary of that and scanned the stations until he found one that played hard rock, though even that was too tame for him. He preferred more hardcore metal and industrial, specifically German industrial which didn't amuse his drill sergeant when he'd overheard it during boot camp.

"Jesus Christ, how the fuck did you ever pass the psychological! You some kind of Nazi lover?"

He said he wasn't, which was true. Though there were aspects of the Nazi party the Scorpion did admire. Especially Himmler's proficiency at purging the country of undesirables.

A good two hours passed when a black Explorer with an Uber sticker pulled in. Kaylee came out wearing a brunette wig. *Clever.* She tossed a backpack in the backseat and got in. With no tracking, the Scorpion followed but kept a safe distance.

The Uber went north until it connected to Las Vegas Boulevard and stayed there until it reached a roadside motel near Nellis Air Force Base. The place was hard to miss with the giant cartoon satellite that looked more like an alien spaceship that read Welcome to the Satellite Motel glowing against the graying dusk-filled surroundings.

The Scorpion drove past the motel and into an adjacent lot with a small 24-hour bar that offered cheap cocktails and video poker. He parked where he had a good view of the motel entrance across a patch of lava rock and palms.

He went to a small diner named Ralph's nearby and got a chicken sandwich and coffee to go. There was no movement when he got back. The parking lot to the motel had the same late model junkers parked there as before he left.

The food helped, and the coffee was surprisingly

better than the motor oil he'd been getting lately. A satisfied stomach made the time go by. He'd learned tricks in the military to keep his mind occupied while doing extended surveillance ops. As the night went on, he tried to get some light sleep. It was the only kind of sleep he ever got. He drifted out for a period until the headlights of an approaching Range Rover roused him.

He checked the time. A little after three. The Rover pulled to the front of the motel and parked. Two well-sized men in sports suits stepped out while leaving the engine running. One was bald with a thick goatee while the slightly shorter, balding one had dark, askew hair.

"Fucking amateurs," the Scorpion cursed, as he watched them go into the front office.

Soon as they were out of sight, the Scorpion slid out of the car, grabbed the sawed-off shotgun and started loading it as the two men came out and started walking toward one of the rooms. The Scorpion moved in on them.

When he passed the front office, he saw a young teen who was managing the front desk sprawled out on the ground with his legs and arms akimbo. His throat had been slit from ear to ear.

The two men used a universal keycard they had taken and swiped it to the door sensor of room 27. Their guns drawn as they swung the door open and went in. Unbeknown to them, the Scorpion was only a few steps behind.

Kaylee was already out of bed with her hands reaching to the ceiling when the Scorpion stuck the sawed-off into the back of the bald goon as he was aiming to shoot Kaylee. The blast nearly split the goon in half as it severed his spine. He fell to the floor and the Scorpion fired another one into his head.

The goatee goon fired but missed. He was at too close a range to aim properly. He opted to foolishly tackle the Scorpion to the wall. The shotgun hit the ground as the Scorpion grabbed the man's gun hand and started bending his fingers backward. A snapping sound, like cracked walnuts caused the man to scream in agony as the gun fell.

The Scorpion kicked the gun and it spun like a pinwheel across the floor as both men jockeyed for position over the other. The Scorpion was stronger and more skilled and overtook the balding man as he slid his right arm underneath his jaw while wrapping his left behind his head. He pulled his shoulders back and started applying pressure which caused the goon to start tapping him as if he thought it was some sanctioned fight. The Scorpion almost started laughing as he leaned back even further and could feel the man's larynx crush. Blood bubbled from his mouth and piddled onto his shirt.

He kept the pressure on for a good amount of time until he was sure the man was dead. He expected Kaylee to have fled during this time but was surprised to see her on the other side of the room with a look of horror and curiosity.

"Let's go," he said as he stood up.

Kaylee pulled her pants on, along with her wig, gathered her things into the backpack she had brought, and followed him out as a BMW came screeching in. *Backup.*

The Scorpion wasted no time as he leapt into the Challenger and punched it before Kaylee could finish shutting the passenger door.

The BMW accelerated at them as the Scorpion roared the machine down the empty boulevard. The high RPMs shook the car and the tires screamed in protest as he started into a sharp right turn. The Scorpion had the feel of the Challenger by now and knew how to dance with it. He let off the gas slightly as it glided on edge before throttling back up. For a few seconds, he was sure a terrified-looking Kaylee thought they were going to flip.

When they cleared the turn, Kaylee looked back in time to see the BMW trying to make the turn. The driver came in too fast, overcompensating, and jerked the wheel in the other direction but it was too late. The BMW jerked hard to the right and flipped end over end. The roof started to cave in on itself like a collapsible tent. It kept summersaulting before landing back on its broke rims and rolled backward in an eerie fashion as if it were a ghost ship being swept to sea.

The Scorpion kept going and soon all that was left to see was smoke of the wreck in the widening distance.

Chapter 17

The police scanner buzzed with cops and responders over the incident. Witnesses reported seeing the Challenger fleeing the area of the downed BMW.

"We got to get this car off the road," the Scorpion said.

Kaylee hadn't said anything during the whole ordeal. Probably still in shock. As they drove through North Vegas, the Scorpion saw what he was looking for. A mid-scale motel with a giant flashing sign with a crescent moon on top that read Sandman Motel. A large arrow pointed to the entrance.

He parked the car between two bigger trucks so it was hidden from the road and started walking toward the entrance of the motel. The Scorpion was halfway across the road when he heard the passenger door open and Kaylee's footsteps following behind him. She had closed the distance by the time he reached the office.

"You don't seem surprised at all that I didn't flee." she said.

"No. You're smart and know I'm your best chance at staying alive."

She scowled and was about to say something, but The Scorpion didn't stand around to listen. He swung the office door open and walked straight toward the large woman with a cherub face working the front desk.

"How long y'all stayin'?" she asked. The Scorpion

was unsure if the twang was legit or not. A lot of people in customer service faked them.

"A couple of days possibly."

"Very good. What kind of room would you like, darlin'?"

He looked the list over and chose Suite-2, which had two queen size beds a mini fridge and a half kitchen.

"What's the Wi-Fi password," Kaylee asked. It was the first time she had spoken up.

"Why, it's guest2335. Not very personable, if you ask me. I've been trying to get them to change it to somethin' more excitin'. This is Vegas, after all."

"Yes, it sure is," Kaylee said, taking one of the key cards.

Room 58 was in the back courtyard facing the pool. Kaylee opened the door, went straight to one of the queens and collapsed. The Scorpion stood in the doorway looking over the room. The carpet was filthy. The beds and linens were worn out. There was a coffee can in one of the cabinets but no pot and a desk but no chair. The bathroom was small with chunks of tile missing and no soap in the shower stall.

He shut the door, set his duffel down, and went straight to the wet bar. At least that was stocked. He grabbed the ice bucket, walked out the door, down the hall, and filled it. He returned to the room, dumping a few cubes into a glass, and emptied two bottles of bourbon into it. He walked over to window, staring out through the curtains.

He could hear the air horn of the Union Pacific locomotive in the distance. It wasn't loud enough to where it would make sleep impossible but enough you could hear the cars full of coal rumbling and shaking in the distance. He sipped his drink and tried to think of what to do next. By tomorrow, the entire city would be gunning for him.

****

The Satellite Motel was swarming with cops and trying to keep a clean crime scene was nearing impossible for Detective Chase. The shootout and chase had brought in every cop in the city. The media was all over it. Things all of a sudden had gotten very real. So much so the sheriff of Clark County himself asked Chase to bring him up to speed on his suspected hitman before addressing the media.

What a mess. The two dead in the motel were Armenian muscle, and so were the two bodies they pulled out of the flipped BMW. The one that had been shot in the back was identified as Gor Sahakian and had a whole list of priors along with connections to Armenian Power aka the Armenian mob. Same with the one with the crushed larynx and even though the two in the BMW hadn't been identified yet, it was a pretty good bet they were Armenian thugs as well.

"The room was checked out to a Miss Judy Garland," McCarthy said.

Chase grunted. "Cute."

McCarthy looked at the sawed-off shotgun they found next to one of the bodies. "Close range shotgun, just like the tweaker. Think we got two different perps?"

Chase shook his head. "No. But I'm sure he'd like us to think that. He's simply using the best weapon for the job."

"I'm starting to hate dealin' with professionals."

"Me, too."

Chase was alone in thinking it was one suspect. The variation of weapons and randomness had other detectives convinced they were dealing with multiple suspects. But it wasn't random at all.

Most crimes it was easy to separate the suspects. It was always the overlap in the Venn diagram where things got tricky. And this guy knew it. He wasn't trying to get away with anything. Just stir up enough confusion and mayhem that by the time the dust settled, and they were able to sort it out, he'd be gone.

****

The Scorpion left Kaylee sleeping as he walked to the diner to get something to eat. He ordered a Denver omelet and sat at the counter. The few patrons there at that time all looked hung over from the night before. He ordered a stack of pancakes and bacon and another cup of coffee to go. When he got back to the room, Kaylee was awake. She was sitting up in bed with the television on. It was tuned to the local news, and all they were talking about was the downed BMW and two dead guys in it along with the Satellite Motel killings.

The Scorpion handed her the box of pancakes and bacon which she ate unhesitatingly. He stood sipping his coffee and watched what the media was reporting. They didn't know much. No suspects yet. Possibly a Dodge Challenger involved. They cut to a police spokesman who said a lot without saying anything. Which meant he was good at his job.

"Why did you help me?" Kaylee asked. She had finished her food and was staring at him.

"I need you to find the guys I intend to kill," he said.

The stoic, matter-of-fact manner he said it caught Kaylee off guard. "Who are they?"

"People that owe me money."

Kaylee laughed. "You mean the guys that hired you. So much for honor among thieves."

The Scorpion didn't say anything. Instead, he contemplated if he really did need her. As if seeing the wheels turning in his head, Kaylee interrupted.

"I can help. I'm very good with computers."

"Yeah?"

"Yes. Soon as I finish college, my dad was going to have me handle that aspect of his investigations."

The Scorpion studied her intensely and saw that she was telling the truth. He opened the canvas duffel and tossed her the pawn shop owner's phone.

"Think you can get into the phone?"

She turned it on and examined it for a moment. "PIN protection can be tricky but it looks like an older operating system, which there are some tricks you can do, but I'll need the person's information…"

He tossed her the pawn shop owner's wallet. She flipped it open and pulled out his driver's license. "So, this is Mr. Chet Keesey's phone?"

The Scorpion said nothing. He never asked or cared about who he was.

"You killed him, didn't you?"

His silence answered her question. "You don't care at all, do you? It's just about the money, right?"

He continued to ignore her questions and drank his coffee while fighting off the itch to make her shut-up.

"Fine," she stated with a sigh. "I'll see what I can do."

"Don't do it here," he said. "There's a strip mall

nearby. Get on their Wi-Fi and do it."

"What are you going to do?"

"Find another car."

Chapter 18

Along East Sahara Avenue was an assortment of used car lots. The Scorpion got off the SX bus and walked along the dealerships. He wasn't worried at all about the girl fleeing or going to the cops while he was gone. She seemed smart enough to know he was the best chance she had at surviving whoever was after her. Not only that, she had seen firsthand what he was capable of.

He kept on the sidewalk, past lava rock landscapes, auto part stores, smog check kiosks, and drive-thru hamburger joints until he found the lot he was looking for. Viva Motors. The salesman on hand looked unscrupulous enough not to ask for a lot of paperwork. The Scorpion didn't need long to browse the lot to find what he was looking for.

"Got your eye on the 2003 Lexus GS430," the salesman said in a singsong voice.

"That's right."

"Great choice, if I might say."

"You wouldn't be much use at your job if you said otherwise."

The salesman frowned at the remark. He was tall, lean, in a tight polyester suit, spotted tie, and a tacky painter's brush mustache.

The Scorpion popped the hood so he could get a look at the V8 engine. Unlike American built V8s, this one had more power to it, making the vehicle a lot faster than it looked. The ideal sleeper car.

The salesman grinned like a Cheshire cat. "Pretty powerful car, if I might say. Sure, there are cars on the lot that look helluva lot faster but soon as you pop the hood, you come to find out they got nothing but sewing machines for engines."

"How much?"

"The sticker says $2,500."

"I'm not asking what the sticker says; I want to know how much you are willing to give up to make this sale."

"Mister, I don't need to make this sale."

"Sure you do. I've been watching this place for half an hour. Nobody has even shown the slightest sign of interest. I bet if I check your books, you haven't made a sale in weeks."

"$2,000 is as low as I can go."

"I'll give you $1,900, cash. Take it or leave it."

He was dangling fresh meat out in front of a feral dog. The salesman couldn't resist.

"Let's go inside."

The Scorpion smirked as he followed the salesman to his office, his head sinking lower with each step.

****

The offsite detective bureau on W. Cheyenne Avenue was full with detectives. Some of them Detective Chase had never even seen before. It didn't matter how many they brought in, everything was leading to dead ends.

Chase was re-checking every interview conducted in an attempt to find something. The server at Ralph's diner that was near the motel might have seen a man come in prior to the shootout.

Jake Weilder—DOB: 03-14-98—is an employee of Ralph's Diner, 4437 Las Vegas Blvd. He was working at the time of 2100-0500 of 01/9.

Weilder stated the following:

-A WMA came in a few hours before the shooting at the Satellite Motel. Height approximately 6 feet, weight approximately 160-175 pounds. Hair short brown/blond?

-Heard gunshots coming from the direction of the hotel at approx. 0310 of 01/10.

-Did not see anyone. Heard tires screeching shortly after.

Not seeing very much was a common theme with all the witnesses they found. A car passing by spotted a Dodge Challenger driving away from the wrecked BMW. Did not see driver due to rate of speed. The partial plate by another witness turned out to be more guess work than him remembering.

ATF was looking at the sawed-off shotgun, but Chase knew nothing would come of it. Forensics had pulled up dozens of fingerprints at the motel but none of them matched any known prints when ran through the databases.

If that wasn't bad enough, the usual flow of information seemed to be almost non-existent. He was still waiting on a court order to get the dead pawn shop owner's phone records. If he didn't know better, it seemed someone was purposely trying to gum up the works.

Chase's only bit of hope came from a call from the North LV station. They picked up a Kevin Mercer for armed robbery; holding up a casino cage at gun point.

He stated upon his arrest he had information on the pawn shop murder.

An officer was standing over Mercer in the interview room when Chase walked in. A few years back, a murder suspect cuffed to the table managed to break the cuffs and escape through the ceiling. It took several days and a lot of bad publicity before he was recaptured. From that point on, suspects were never left alone.

Mercer was skinny, long brown hair, scraggily goatee. His eyes were bloodshot. *Drugs.*

"You said you have some information on the murder of Chet Keesey?" Chase asked.

"Sure I do. But I want a deal."

'Course he did.

"I don't make deals. You either tell me what you know, or you can go back to jail. It's that simple."

Mercer just looked at him.

"Could you at least put something down that I cooperated with you. Might help me with the judge."

"Possibly. No guarantees. What do you know?"

He rubbed his chin with his free hand and leaned back.

"I worked for Keesey at the pawn shop. Except it wasn't much of a pawn shop. More like his side job."

"What was his real job?"

"He did business with all kinds of shady people. Dealers, casinos, you name it. He had connections, and so they went to him to make deals."

"What kind of deals?" Chase asked.

"Any kind of deal you can think of."

"You mean, like murder? He hire a contract killer?"

Mercer laughed. "He done and hired the devil himself is what he did."

"Why?"

"Some powerful guys wanted him to. I don't know who. He never said."

"And you think this hired killer is the one that killed Keesey?"

"I know he did."

"Why?"

Mercer leaned forward in his chair. "Because Keesey told me that he was told by the boys he was working for that as soon as the jobs were done he had to close the loop."

"Let me get this straight. They wanted him to kill the professional killer?"

"That's right."

"You expect me to buy this?"

"Yessir, I do. Because it's the God's honest truth."

Chase started to massage his temples. He needed to stew on this.

"Officer, you can escort Mr. Mercer back to his cell."

Chapter 19

The room was empty except for the sound of running water. The Scorpion looked around and saw the bathroom door open. Steam was coming out. He stepped closer and saw Kaylee's dark, curvy silhouette through the shower curtain. A bracelet-covered wrist protruded through the thin curtain as she rested a hand against the shower wall.

He turned away and grabbed a few vodka bottles off the cabinet and lay down on one of the beds, staring up at the ceiling. He listened to the whirring of the air conditioning and thought about nothing in particular until her singing brought his attention back to the open bathroom door.

Her shadow moved with the kind of grace that came from years of ballet and showed that Tolstoy was right when he wrote that all beauty of life was made up of light and shadows.

He could sense her standing over him. He opened his eyes. She was dressed, but her wavy red hair was still damp.

"I was able to get into the phone," she said. "I got into his account and used Find My Device to reset the PIN. I archived everything on the device on my laptop."

The Scorpion nodded. He knew she had done more than just that. He was right. She had taken the time also to call Toney to see how her dad was doing.

"Nothing's changed," he told her. He sounded worried. "Are you okay? Why haven't you come to see him?"

"I'm caught up in something right now. I'll tell you more later." He tried to press her for more, but she told him to just trust her before hanging up.

"We can look at it later," the Scorpion said. "First, we got to dispose of the car."

Half an hour later, the Scorpion hopped in the Challenger still sandwiched between two SUVs and out of view from the street. Kaylee got in the Lexus. He had instructed her that if he was to be stopped by police not to follow but meet him back at the motel instead.

He turned the scanner on and drove slowly, following the speed limit before getting on 1-15 South. He stayed on the highway for twenty or so miles before taking NV-161 toward Goodsprings. He remembered this route from the last time he was in Vegas. His gun buyer had taken him there to go shooting. Kaylee was still behind him as he turned left onto Sandy Valley Road. It was getting dark as they went through Columbia Pass, which went between the Spring and Table Mountain ranges.

From there they reached a ten mile stretch of road where dozens of ore and copper mines and starter shafts were located. The Scorpion pulled off the road toward one of them. The Challenger rocked and shimmied from the rough terrain as it smashed through Mojave Desert cactus until he dipped into a small rocky valley secluded from the road. He stopped in front of the entrance to a mine in the side of a small hill.

It was now dark enough to where Kaylee kept the headlights on the Challenger for light. He took a screwdriver from the glove box and yanked out the VIN plate from the push-pin rivets on the dash. He took the police scanner and the rest of his gear from the trunk of the car and switched it to the Lexus. Next, he got out a five-gallon gas can he had filled up at a filling station earlier and doused the inside of the Challenger with it before tossing an ignited roadside flare into the open driver side window.

It took only seconds for the vehicle to become fully engulfed in flames. The Scorpion had torched enough cars to know that the hood, doors, and hatches could explode open with a lot of force at any time. He didn't stand around long to watch it burn.

Kaylee had switched to the passenger seat when he got to the car again. He could see her watching the flames with the same look she'd had when he was strangling a man to death.

He reversed and headed back to the main road. No one would see the fire, and by the time someone found the car, it'd just be a husk of burnt metal. Even if they pulled the VIN from the engine block and traced it to the rental agency, all they would find was a fake ID of some dead person he'd ghosted.

Nobody would remember him. Not even the security guard in the garage noticed him. He was playing some game on his phone and just glanced at the paperwork and opened the gate. He was no different than most people today, a bug following the hive with no clue on what was really going on around them until it was too late.

Chapter 20

It was quiet except for the continuous beeping of the cardiac monitor. Roddick's heartrate held steady at 77 with a CO2 reading of 98.

Detective Chase stared down at him. His vitals seemed fine.

Toney was sitting beside him watching the Golden Knights play the LA Kings on television. He stood up as soon as he saw Chase.

"How's he doing?" Chase asked.

"Same. Nobody knows when or if he'll wake up."

"He will. Where's his daughter?"

Toney hesitated. "She goes to college. She'll see him later this week."

Chase wondered what was behind the hesitation but decided to let it go.

"Look, I wanted to apologize for the way I acted the other night," Toney said. "I was a real asshole. I'm just on edge seeing Joe like this."

"I understand. You two were close."

"Very. We were partners. You know how that goes."

Chase nodded. "Yes, I suppose I do."

"Listen, the game is over, and I was going to grab a coffee on my way out. Let me buy you one, least I can do for the way I acted."

"Sure, why not?"

The Black Cow Café was conveniently located inside the hospital near the front entrance. They both ordered the house brew with no sugar.

"You must have your hands full," Toney said, setting the coffee down at a vacant table. "Double homicide in a roadside motel, another two killed in a high speed shootout not far away."

"It's a damn war zone. I tell you, it seems like this town is going to hell."

"Well, it is Vegas. What'd you expect?"

"Not this. Sure, we get the gang shootings and homicides like any city this size. It just seems recently the amount of killing going on has accelerated."

"What you got here is nothing," Toney said. "Shit, when we were working Providence, it had the highest murder rate in all of New England. Just isolated events here. It'll blow over."

"That might be true, but this kind of stuff scares tourists away, and that's not good for a town that runs off of tourism."

"Good point. You got a suspect in that motel shooting yet?"

"Yes. We think it's the same professional that shot Roddick."

Toney swallowed too much of the scalding coffee and burnt the roof of his mouth. He winced in pain

"No shit?"

"To be honest, I've never come across a suspect like this. The calculated ruthlessness. The skill."

"Say, you ever heard of Maury Lerner?"

Chase shook his head.

"He was a triple-A ballplayer back in the '50s. Had a batting average of .364. Man, he could hit, my old man would tell me. Athletic as hell and always stayed in top shape too, unlike most of them ballplayers in that time. But he had a nasty side to him. When his ball career started going nowhere, he went to work for Providence crime boss Raymond Patriarca. Soon bodies started piling up, and the police got to hearing word about this athletic, handsome hitman called the Pro."

"What happened to him?"

"What always happens to guys like that—someone ratted him out. Got sent up to the Rhode Island Adult Correctional Institution. Became a model inmate, got out in '88 and moved here to Vegas. Died a few years back."

"You know, I think I remember reading something about that. Spent his last years helping out his son's law firm of all things."

"That's right."

"You think I got one these guys on my hands?"

Toney shrugged. "Maybe."

****

Kaylee was in her element, sitting in front of her laptop with a cold energy drink and pizza. She was going through screenshots of Keesey's phone log she'd archived on her laptop. The Scorpion was on other side of the room, flipping through channels on television until he settled on an old spaghetti western.

"He deleted all his text messages but got and made a lot of calls from a 702-847-2298."

With almost indifference, he said, "Get me the name and address."

She glared up at him, but he wasn't paying attention to her. His nonchalant demeanor annoyed her. He was the reason her dad was laid up in a hospital bed with the real chance of never waking up and he could care less. The only time she saw any emotion from him was when he was killing people.

She knew he was dangerous and that was what she needed. She had no problem with him using her, mostly for bait, because she needed him to take care of whoever wanted her dead. In a perverted way, they were both using each other.

She searched the number on social media and then a paid reverse directory site her dad used and got a hit.

"Okay, I got it."

This got the Scorpion's attention. She was startled by how fast he had shut the television off and was standing next to her.

"Who is it?" he asked.

Chapter 21

It'd been a rough couple of days for Frank Valentas. Sure, he got promoted to operations manager, but he would have preferred to have gotten it without having a pal like Lockhart being stuffed into the trunk of his car.

The police questioning him about what happened was bad enough. Now he had dead Armenians and some psycho hitman on the loose.

He sipped his dry martini and tried to relax. He was sitting at the 107 Sky Lounge in the Stratosphere Tower with some friends, who also ran operations in several casinos. It was sunset, and you couldn't beat the 360-degree view of the city. The street lights below twinkled against the last bits of glimmering sunlight in the valley.

"You won't believe who came to see me today," one of them said.

"Who?"

"That son of a bitch Robert Deirde!"

Deirde was a lawyer who had made a name for himself as the go-to attorney for gamblers. More specifically, gamblers roughed up by security.

"What the hell did he want?"

"To tell me he was representing some card counter I threw out a few months ago. Said it'd be in the casino's and my best interests to settle."

" 'Course he did. What'd you do to the guy?"

"Not a goddamn thing. Physically, at least. We just went into his room while he was running a train on some whores and threw them all out on the street."

That got a laugh out of all of them.

"Awfully quiet tonight, Frank? The wife mad you're not home?"

"Naw," Frank said. "She dragged the boy to go see some play at the Smith Center tonight."

"Christ, what is it with women and the performing arts? And traveling for that matter. Why do they always want to travel to some resort in some shithole country?"

"So they can snap a bunch of selfies and post them on social media and make all their dumb friends jealous, I suppose."

"I hate traveling. Every time I've gone out of the country I've gotten sick from the awful food or contaminated water and spent most of the trip locked up in the bathroom. Waste of fucking money is what it is."

They kept at it and Frank listened. The meaningless chatter along with the alcohol and mellow background music a DJ was putting on seemed to have calmed his nerves. He checked his watch. They wouldn't be home for a few hours.

A quiet house once in a while was something to look forward to, so he called it an early night and left to head to his gated community home in Summerlin. It was a well-off area, with most residents behind gates to keep the riff-raff out. His place was no exception. It was a two-story, five bedroom stucco house at the end of a cul-de-sac.

He turned the lights on as soon as he got in and went straight to the kitchen to pour himself another drink. That's when he saw him.

Someone was standing in the doorway that went into the dining room, holding a Glock to his side and something else in his other hand.

"How'd you find me?"

The Scorpion didn't respond.

"I can get you the rest of your money, if that's what you're after."

"I'm after more than that now."

"Look, I don't make the decisions."

" 'Course you don't. You're too dumb to be making the decisions. I want to know the man who got the idea to break the arrangement."

"I don't know who that would be."

The Scorpion held up a family photo of Valentas' wife and son.

"I could wait until they come back. Maybe they would know."

"Fuck—"

The Scorpion shot him twice in the chest before he could finish and stood over him as he bled out on the hardwood floor.

"The Armenians are coming for you, you fuck."

The Scorpion didn't respond as he fired another round into his head.

****

Kaylee knew as soon as he walked in he had killed someone. He said nothing to her, as usual, and went straight to the bathroom. He took his shirt off and ran water over his face. When he turned around, she saw the Iron Cross necklace and the tattoo on his lower left shoulder.

"Why do you have a scorpion tattoo?"

He was midway from putting on another shirt when he stopped. Kaylee immediately regretted asking. He stood there, thinking. She could tell he was deciding whether or not it was worth keeping her around. A mixture of embarrassment and anger at him started to come over her but she pushed it down into her stomach, to be dealt with at a later date.

He finished dressing and stretched out on the other bed. Kaylee scowled at him. Nothing bothered this bastard while her nerves couldn't be any more on the edge without sanity falling off. She could never tell when he was sleeping or not. Any time she stepped close to his bed she could see his eyes flicker, warning her not to come any closer.

She sat down on her bed and thought about the scorpion tattoo; a skull for a head and claws open. She went on her phone and found that the open claws on a scorpion tattoo usually meant a military person who had seen combat.

She glanced at him and could only imagine the amount of death he must have taken part in. Yet here he was, unfazed.

Chapter 22

It took a while to calm the wife down. She had called 911 after coming home with her son and finding her husband lying in a pool of blood the size of Lake Meade on the kitchen floor.

The homicide didn't catch Detective Chase's interest until he was tipped off the deceased had taken over Lockhart's job at the Lucky Hearts Casino. Before he left to the scene, he grabbed a copy of the interview Valentas had given to Detective McCarthy a few days prior in regards to Lockhart's murder.

Chase stood in the kitchen and looked over the interview as the same forensic investigator from the medical examiner's office that had handled Rivera's body, worked on Valentas.

Valentas had told McCarthy he had no idea who would want to kill Lockhart. That Lockhart being murdered had completely caught him off guard. When asked how he seemed to benefit from Lockhart's misfortune, he denied any wrong-doing. Said he was close to Lockhart and he honestly didn't want the promotion.

As they bagged Valentas' body, Chase wondered if he knew the promotion would end this way.

"Wifey finally settled down," McCarthy said. "Had her go through the house, see if anything was missing. Said a bottle of Vicodin her husband got a month ago after having a root canal was gone, along with a package of shaving razors, and some mouthwash."

"He didn't take the cell phone this time," Chase said.

"Maybe he found what he was looking for?"

"I'd hate to imagine what that could be."

"We need to shake down the Lucky Hearts Casino and see what this is about."

"Good luck," Chase said. "They'll lawyer up. They always do."

"Don't you think this is different? That they know it's in their best interest and this town's to get this nut off the front page and scaring tourists away?"

"You'd think, but they won't see it that way," Chase said. "Dealt with them enough to know they like to handle things internally."

"That's all we need now. More hired guns coming in."

"I got a feeling they're already here."

****

The Scorpion left early, saying something about needing more firepower. He had given Kaylee some money to get food. She was glad he was gone. She had done some extra digging the previous day in Keesey's call log and found another number he called regularly. It was, in fact, the last call he made.

Through reverse-directory search, she found it belonged to a Scarlett Hewitt. An online search through her social media platforms revealed she was a burlesque dancer at The Lusty Lady, off Sammy Davis Jr Drive. From their webpage, she was scheduled to dance later that afternoon.

She took the 201 bus to Tropicana and Maryland

and walked the rest of the way to the UNLV campus. Though she had missed a few classes, she emailed her teachers telling them she needed time off because of her dad and they all seemed pretty understanding for the most part.

Her dorm was empty, which suited her. Her roommate Jessica was obnoxious. She was the girly-girl type that always annoyed Kaylee. The constant need to gossip about things Kaylee could care less about. If Jessica was there, she'd want to get all up in Kaylee's business, which she was in no mood for.

Kaylee showered, changed her clothes from her usual casual jeans and t-shirt to an older looking low-cut dress. She used two bras, a trick she learned from a girl she knew who worked at Hooters, to amplify her cleavage. Next, she did her makeup so it made her look a little bit older to pass for being 21.

Though it was risky if she was still being watched, she retrieved her car and drove to grab some food at a nearby convenience store, then headed to the club, arriving a little before noon.

Between sips of her energy drink, she gathered her nerve and followed a group of young men. The doorman didn't even bother carding her or asking for the fifty-dollar cover fee. The perks of being an attractive female.

Though it was the middle of the afternoon, the club was well packed with fans of the old school style of strip tease that was burlesque. The girls on stage wore corsets and were doing sultry removals of their long gloves and garter belts. The tricks of the trade. Though most strip clubs in Vegas were only topless because Nevada Law didn't allow fully nude establishments to serve alcohol, the girls on stage kept it classy when they removed their tops with strategically placed pasties. This suited Kaylee, who didn't mind seeing the dancing but not the other forms of debauchery that came with modern day stripping.

She found an empty table as far from the main stage as possible. A waitress in fishnets and 7-inch platforms came by to take her order. Kaylee ordered a Fireball. She needed to loosen up.

Hewitt, who went by the stage name Lady Desire, came on the stage with two large fans made of ostrich and marabou feathers. She was a pretty girl. Tall, long blonde hair dyed in a pink and purple unicorn tint.

The waitress came back with her shot and Kaylee downed it. The spicy cinnamon felt good and seemed to relax her. She watched as Hewitt seductively wooed and teased the crowd with her fan dance. When it was finished, Kaylee discreetly approached the stage before Hewitt could leave.

"You're a great dancer."

The woman snapped her gum.

"Thanks, sweetie."

"Do you know a Chet Keesey?"

She stopped snapping.

"Yes. Why?"

"He's dead."

The news seemed to catch her by surprise.

"Look, I got to get backstage. Stick around; I'll be back out in a few minutes."

"Okay."

Kaylee ordered another Fireball as she waited. Several dancers were chatting up on stage with the customers throwing dollar bills at them like confetti.

Hewitt spotted her not long after and took a seat across from Kaylee, crossing her long legs, and smoking.

"You must make a lot doing this," Kaylee said.

"Not as much as you'd think. It costs a lot having to maintain. Nails, hair, makeup, clothes."

"Can't you itemize any of that?"

Hewitt laughed. "Sure, I'll get right on that next time I bother filling out a 1099."

The same waitress came by with a vodka martini for Hewitt.

"See those girls over there?" Hewitt asked.

Kaylee turned to strippers chatting it up with the two men.

"That's where the money is. The regulars. Those same guys come in every week and drop thousands on those same two girls."

"Why?"

"Because men are born suckers when it comes to sex. They got no control over their dicks. None."

"I suppose."

Hewitt took a moment to study Kaylee's face.

"You're a little young, aren't you? How do you know Chet?"

"I don't," Kaylee said. "I just happen to have his phone."

"Why do you have his phone?"

"It's a long story."

"I'm in no hurry."

"First tell me, what's your relationship with him?"

Hewitt laughed. "My relationship? Listen, sweetie, Chet was a perv like all the rest. But a well-paying one. Always bought me things, so sometimes I'd do things for him. Get what I'm saying."

"Yes, I think I do. Did he ever talk about what he did?"

"For work? Yeah, he ran some pawn shop. But that's not how he made his money. He was a glorified errand boy for some big-time criminals, but if you ask him, it was him calling the shots."

"You never believed he was?"

"Chet was a moron. A well-connected moron. Now, how do you happen to have his phone?"

"I got it from the person who killed him."

Hewitt's eyes flickered as she mashed the remainder of her cigarette in the ashtray "You don't say. He your boyfriend or something?"

"I don't think so. I'm pretty sure he's going to try and kill me when the time is right."

"Why're you with him?"

"I need him to take care of some guys that want to kill me first. Why I came to see you. Did Chet talk to you about who he was working for recently?"

Hewitt thought about it and shook her head. "No, honey, I can't say. The last time I saw him, he just talked about how he's moving up and will be making real money. I think he was trying to convince me to be with him."

"You didn't know he was killed, did you."

"No."

"You don't watch the news?"

"Not anymore, no. It's all fake."

Kaylee nodded and started to stand.

"Hey, give me your number and let me ask a few other girls he flirted around with. Maybe they know something."

Kaylee wrote the number down on a cocktail

napkin. "I got my phone ringer off most of the day, so text me."

"Will do, sweetie," Hewitt said as she stuffed the napkin into her bra.

Chapter 23

Kaylee dropped her car back off on campus and caught the bus to the motel before the Scorpion showed up.

When he did, he said nothing except to ask if she had eaten. She said she had, so he went back to watching television the remainder of the evening.

He left again the next day saying he had more supplies to get. She didn't want to know what he was stockpiling such an arsenal for.

Several times she thought about leaving but whoever wanted her dead would find her, or he would.

She tried to relax but couldn't. She hated waiting for things to happen. She took a walk and checked her phone. That's when the text from Hewitt showed up: *Talked with another girl that knew Chet. Told me some things I think you'd be interested in. Meet me later.*

Kaylee texted back, and seconds later Hewitt sent an address to meet up at six.

It was nearly four now. Kaylee went back to the motel, changed into a dress she had brought, put on some makeup, then headed out. But not before leaving a note behind for a certain someone so he knew where she was.

The address she was given was to one of the secret places casinos gave out to VIPs. This one was a hidden villa with a private, gated entrance. The guard at the gate, an older, sweet looking man, smiled when she said Hewitt invited her.

"Yes, of course," he said, punching in the code to the wrought-iron gate. It swung open to a private pool area with marble statues. She recognized several strippers from the previous day dancing with hairy, tattooed, East European men who looked similar to the ones that showed up at her motel. She neared the water that glowed a florescent purple and saw several girls swimming nude. What had she walked in to?

Around the pool area were Chinese Chippendale-style lounge chairs that sat empty as the Slovak men squatted Gopnik-style in groups with their hands hanging from their knees while holding cigarettes or half-empty bottles of beer. It was a bizarre sight to see.

"Hey, sweetie."

Kaylee turned and saw Hewitt standing on the patio. "Glad you could make it. Come back here, it's quieter."

She took Kaylee's hand and led her through the crowded bungalow that was full of more tattooed East European men smoking and talking.

Toward the back was a pool table where an assortment of men standing around while a big one with greasy, slicked black hair sized up his shot. Kaylee could tell he was the one in charge.

"Egor, this is her," Hewitt said.

Kaylee yanked her hand free.

"Sorry, sweetie. He didn't leave me much of a choice."

"Go," Egor said. Hewitt left. He turned to the rest of his sleazy acolytes, who realized he meant them as well and they cleared out.

"Want anything? A drink?"

Kaylee shook her head.

"Relax, I'm not interested in killing you anymore. I just want him, understand?"

"Yes."

"I never met him, you know, but the ones of us that have all ended up dead. So I don't even know what he looks like."

"Do you want me to tell you, is that why you brought me here?"

"I brought you here for more than that."

"He won't come for me."

"I think he will. The fact you are still alive tells me you hold some kind of interest of his, no?"

"He's only using me to get to you. I'm simply bait, nothing more."

"See, he will come. Maybe not for you, but for me. His revenge."

****

He sat parked in front of the motel for a moment, listening to the hum of the cooling fan, and took stock of his inventory. The Scorpion had dealings with the Armenians before in SoCal. He'd spoken with a few contacts who told him the man in charge of the Vegas operations was some Russian named Egor.

He used the remainder of what he had been paid so far to get two more Glocks, another shotgun, and lots of ammunition, along with Type IIIA body armor and plating. An added bonus was he got his hands on some explosives. As soon as he found the Armenian's stronghold, he intended to use it to blow them straight to hell.

He got to the room and stopped. There was no

sound coming from inside. He took out his Glock and hugged the corner as he opened the door. Nothing. He checked the bathroom and found no one. Did she make a break for it? There would have been cops here if she had. He set the gun down and started taking off his coat before he saw the note underneath the remote for the television.

****

They kept playing pool as she watched. Egor switched between speaking in Russian and Armenian with each different group of men that would talk with him. They didn't pay her any attention, and she wanted to keep it that way.

Hewitt came by to try and talk but Kaylee was still burned from Hewitt's betrayal.

"Don't be mad," she said. "I'm helping you out. They wanted you dead, but now they just want the guy you're with. It'll all be over soon, promise."

Kaylee rolled her eyes. "Sure."

Hewitt let her be, and Kaylee kept watching them play. She thought about playing pool with her dad. Would she ever be able to again? Even if she made it out okay, he was probably never going to wake up.

She felt tears welling up, and before she could fight to hold them back, a loud explosion shook the house. Screams followed by rapid-fire subsonic shots. Another explosion. Egor and the two men he was playing with rushed outside. More gunfire erupted, another deafening bang with glass shattering. Stray bullets started spraying the walls. Women screamed and ran. Kaylee ducked under the pool table. Men groaned in pain. The gunfire kept going. Would it ever stop? Kaylee covered her ears. She still could feel the vibrations of something exploding. Then nothing.

Kaylee lifted her hands from ears and heard nothing but dead silence. She crawled out from under the table and looked around. The glass door that led to the patio was blown out. She stepped outside. Chunks of patio were missing, leaving only smoldering holes. Bodies lay everywhere. The smell of gunpowder and resin scorched her nostrils. Ejected bullet casings littered the ground and made a crunching sound as she walked over them. Some of the girls had been caught in the crossfire. The pink-purple hair of one of them caught her eye. Hewitt's body lay motionless near the pool. An outstretched arm reached out into the water. Her vacant, dead eyes looked at something off in the distance. Out of the corner of her eye Kaylee saw movement.

Shell shocked, she turned and saw him standing near the entrance. He was in full body armor with his gun to his side and breathing heavily. Upon seeing her, he turned and started slowly walking away. Like a zombie she followed. The front entrance gate had been blown wide open, and the hinges were barely holding it up. The older man that had let her in earlier was face down. As she walked by, she saw that a chunk of his head was missing.

She vomited as she got to the street. She could hear the sound of approaching sirens, but could no longer stand. She swayed, fell to her knees, then retched again. The last thing she saw before she passed out was a pair of combat boots on the ground in front of her.

Chapter 24

It was mid-morning when she woke up screaming. The Scorpion was re-packing his canvas duffel bag and gave no attention to her distress. He was still deciding what to do about her. He should have killed her last night. She'd served her purpose. But for some reason, he didn't and he was trying to figure out why.

When he did bother to look at her, she was sitting up in her bed breathing hard, saturated in sweat. He could tell she was disoriented. It took her a moment to realize where she was. She looked down and saw she was wearing the same blood and vomit-stained clothes she had been wearing the night before. The Scorpion had just tossed her on top of the bed and left her there. When she saw him looking at her, she blurted, "What *are* you?"

He didn't answer but turned and walked into the bathroom. The body armor had held up against the direct shots but left him with bruised ribs. He swallowed a Vicodin from the bottle he had stolen from Valentas and collected his toothbrush, paste, and razor. That's when he heard the familiar click of the Voodoo slide. He pivoted and caught Kaylee pointing the Glock at him. She had taken it out of his bag and from the way she was holding it, she had fired guns before. Daddy must have seen to it.

He didn't bother raising his hands but instead

111

slowly started walking toward her. She fired. He jerked and took the round in his left shoulder. Ignoring the pain, he kept walking. So she shot him in the leg. He tried to shift his weight to the other leg but couldn't and fell, landing on his back.

She straddled over him, still pointing his gun at him, and knelt further down so that she was sitting on his chest with all her weight. He struggled to breathe.

"You may have saved my life, but you still shot my dad," she snarled. "Sooner or later you'd have killed me, too."

He could feel her warm breath as she leaned in and said, "But I am sorry."

She got up off him grabbed her things. He didn't try to stop her. He just looked up at the ceiling as she left.

****

The city needed a break. The mass shooting at the private villa proved to be the tipping point. When it was learned most of the victims were Armenian criminals, strippers, and known prostitutes, all the recent killings were lumped into an isolated case of East European gang warfare that culminated in the massacre.

Detective Chase's superiors seemed to push for that narrative, along with his fellow detectives. The media, by the looks of it, went along with it. Why wouldn't they? They knew these high profile killings weren't good for anyone in town. Sure, once in a while it was good for ratings but not for it to be a recurring thing. It was better to pin it all on gang violence ending with them killing each other than some unknown boogeyman killer still lurking out there.

It mattered little that ballistics had the killings at

the villa being matched to a single gun, an AR-15. Chase was told to keep looking into the matter, but it would be done secretly. As far as media and anyone else was concerned, there was no single shooter responsible for all of it.

Frustrated, Chase arrived early at the station hoping to figure out the best course of action. He got a break when several calls came in reporting gun shots at a motel. This was followed up by an anonymous web submission to the Crime Stoppers Tip Line, stating the shooter was the gunman they were looking for. That he'd been shot. The tipster gave a general description of the suspect and the car he was driving along with the plate numbers.

Chase, with his SIG 9mm, McCarthy, and a dozen heavily-armed officers converged at the motel and pounded on the door to room 58.

"Police, open up."

With no reply, Chase tried the door. Unlocked. He swung it open and they all moved in fast. The room was empty. There was no indication anyone had been staying there except for the blood stains on the carpet. The twin beds had been stripped. An officer searching the premises found a burning dumpster in the back, which must have been the linens. Chase assumed all the surfaces had been wiped clean of prints.

"Looks like a domestic violence case," McCarthy said. "The lady at the front counter said she checked them in a few nights ago. A medium-sized male and a younger brunette. Betting the brunette shot the guy, who was probably a john who didn't pay up, and then left the anonymous tip just to screw him over some more."

Chase clenched his fists. Damn him! All the bastard needed to do was create some doubt, and it all fell apart. He was being played. They all were.

"Put a BOLO out for the car," Chase said and walked out, not even bothering to hide his disgust.

Chapter 25

Kaylee sat on top of her wooden high-riser bed with her dresser and all her worldly possessions stuffed underneath it. The dorm was empty and quiet except for a girl playing loud music down the hall. Kaylee was too distracted to notice. She had been going through the latest news on her laptop, not finding much; her nerves were raw.

Everywhere she went all she could see was Hewitt. When she was walking between classes, she thought she saw her in the halls. In the courtyard, she saw Hewitt's dangling hand reaching out toward the pool, but it turned out to just be some girl lying in the grass with her boyfriend. If that wasn't enough, she was expecting the police to show up any minute, having found out it was her that had given the anonymous tip. Not that it mattered, they were ruling the shooting a domestic dispute. She should have just gone to the police station and come clean, but that would have implicated her in his killing rampage. Her anxiety over all that had happened got so bad that she started seeing a school counselor, who told her she was showing all the symptoms of PTSD. The twice a week sessions seemed to help. She was given coping techniques like breathing exercises and mindful meditations. Even the talk therapy helped a little, but she had to be careful on what she said. Kaylee only told the counselor what happened to her dad. Not how she got mixed up with the very man that put him into a coma or her biggest fear lately—that he was going to jump out at any minute like some crazed jack-in-the-box and take his revenge out on her.

The door flung open, and Kaylee about screamed. It was her roommate, Jessica.

"Sorry, didn't mean to scare you."

"No, no. It's fine."

"You've been jumpy ever since you came back. This about those weird Russian-looking guys?"

"What Russian guys?"

"They came knocking on the door asking for you. I told them you already left in an Uber."

So that's how they were able to find me.

"Oh," Kaylee said. "They won't be coming anymore."

Jessica gave her a confused look, but Kaylee wasn't going to say it was because they were lying on slabs in the morgue.

"Whatever," she said and walked past her, glancing at the book Kaylee was reading. *Hit-Man: A Technical Manual for Independent Contractors.*

"Why are you reading that?"

"Research."

Kaylee learned the book had been used as a how-to guide in a triple homicide. This led to the publisher destroying almost all existing copies, but with persistence, she'd been able to track a copy down.

Jessica dropped her backpack on her bed, making a loud thud, before turning back to Kaylee.

"Should I be worried?"

" 'Course not, stupid."

Jessica scowled.

"Mmmhmm. How's your dad doing?"

Kaylee shrugged. "No change."

"Listen, some friends and I are going dancing this weekend. You should come."

Kaylee had seen videos of Jessica dancing. Grinding up on a bunch of horny strangers was not her idea of having a good time. Shit-posting on random image boards was how she blew off steam.

"Thanks, but I think I should probably stay with him this weekend. I had to take care of some things so I haven't really been there as much as I should've."

"He'll pull through."

Kaylee hoped so. She needed him to be around.

****

McCarthy arrived at Mr. Dees fifteen minutes after he'd texted he was there. It was a sports bar on Rainbow Boulevard. A popular hot spot for cops, especially the motorcycle unit, which Detective Chase had started his career out in.

He found Chase sitting at the bar, staring at a basketball game on one of the many HD televisions. Without saying a word, he took a seat beside him and ordered a beer from the smoke-show tattooed biker girl dressed in a tight Catholic school girl outfit.

"Usually when you come here it's right before you take a weekend ride into the desert."

"Need to get out of this city for a few days," Chase said. "Clear my head. Besides, brass and the media seem to think everything is wrapped up. It doesn't matter we still don't know how Rivera, his junky pal, Lockhart, Valentas, and the Lucky Hearts Casino were involved with this supposed East European turf war narrative they're going with."

"That's not what's really bothering you though. It's that boogeyman killer."

"What? It doesn't bother you that this guy can come here, kill a bunch of people, create a giant mess and vanish?"

"Sure it does. Speaking of vanishing. Before I headed out, got a call. Highway patrol found the 2003 Lexus parked at the Wendover Rest Area off 93. Also found a dead Hispanic male in the trunk. No ID. Most likely an illegal."

"The vehicle he took no doubt was unregistered. He's probably in Salt Lake by now, or Denver."

"One lead might pan out. The ATF is trying to track the explosives used for the pipe bombs at the villa, and find out where they came from."

Chase shook his head. "It'll be another dead-end. I'm telling you, this cat was military. And if they weren't so bad at releasing fingerprints to the FBI database we might have ID'd him already."

"You'd think we'd learned our lesson with departments not sharing information with each other after 9/11."

"Nothing ever changes."

"Nope. Just your underwear."

Chase laughed. It was the first time it seemed his mood had lifted.

Chapter 26

The first thing he could hear was the noise. A buzzing sound. It annoyed him.

The buzzing turned to murmurs. Someone was talking.

He tried to open his eyes but only managed one of them.

It was blurry.

A woman's voice.

A few moments later a filmy figure was standing over him saying something.

He couldn't make it out. A bright light shined at him. He wanted to shield his eyes but couldn't. It was all too exhausting. Then nothing.

Next time he tried opening his eyes it was darker. He got one eye open and half of the other this time. The same female voice. He could make out pieces of what she was saying. "Eyes...up...stable...can you..." Nothing. It repeated like this several times.

Each time he gradually got his eyes open more, and his vision got less blurry. But that didn't seem to help his disorientation.

He did not know where he was.

How he got there.

The man sitting at the side of the bed. He knew it was a doctor. "Can you squeeze my hand?" he asked.

Sure he could squeeze his hand. What kind of

question was that? He'd give him a squeeze all right. Nothing. He tried again. Only a slight budge.

He focused as hard as he could and with the same type of effort one would use to curl a 100-pound dumbbell. All he got for it was being able to slightly coil his hand.

"Very good," the doctor said. "It's a start."

Fatigue came over him again, and suddenly he was out.

When he awoke, a familiar face was sitting beside him.

"Hey, Dad."

Tears welled up in his eyes. He didn't deserve her. She hugged him, and he wanted to hug her back but couldn't.

"You're going to be okay," she said.

With all the effort he had he made a lopsided smile. Then he was out.

****

Kaylee spent a better part of two weeks at the hospital after classes. She got to know the nurses and doctors well. They even brought in the most comfortable pull back chair for her to sit in. Her dad's recovery was slow. He'd wake up periodically throughout the day.

At first, it was only for a few minutes, but it gradually grew to half an hour then forty-five minutes before he would fall asleep again. A physical therapist and occupational therapist would come by once a day. He was able to move his hands more, and they even sat him up so he could try and balance himself out. His strength grew so he could sit up longer and longer. But it exhausted him to where he would sleep for hours after they were done.

"We got a great rehabilitation facility we're going to send him to," the hospital case worker told her.

By the time he was discharged from the hospital, he was able to move with a walker but unable to talk much.

This appeared to annoy Detective Chase, who first showed up in a motorcycle jacket not long after her dad woke up. It seemed he'd cut his weekend ride short.

"I'll let you know as soon as he's able to talk to you, detective," Kaylee told him.

"I'd appreciate that," he said. She didn't care for Detective Chase much. He was cute for an older man, but his constant chip on his shoulder attitude grew tiresome.

She waited in her car as a nurse wheeled her dad out to the front. With the help of a walker, he was able to get in. The case worker was right; the rehab facility wasn't far. Situated on North Tenaye Way. It was small; 38 beds, but accommodating. He was given a private room so that noise wouldn't overstimulate him. They wanted him well rested for therapy sessions.

Kaylee made sure to bring some clothes for him from home, along with his Bruins hat. He smiled but hardly spoke at first. When he did, it was mostly gibberish. But the speech therapist said he was making great progress. Kaylee finally saw the development when she was leaving at the end of his first week there, and he asked, "You ready to see the game on Saturday?"

"You know I am," she said, trying not to cry.

****

The wind was blowing hard and sounded like an

angry banshee as the sky took on a sinister gray. The flashing vacancy light outside shined into the Scorpion's room. He was lying on the bed motionless. Waiting for the Vicodin kick.

The two gunshot wounds were getting better. Not long after the girl left, he slowly got to his feet. He heated his knife blade on the stove and cauterized the wounds as best he could before he bled out. The Vicodin he had taken only moments earlier for the bruised ribs helped.

He'd managed to strip the bed and wipe things down before leaving. He'd tossed the bed sheets into the dumpster out back and doused them with the remaining alcohol miniatures and lit it up. He was backing out as the first responding officer squealed into the motel.

The Scorpion hit up the first drug store he saw and got some antiseptic and bandages and patched himself up in the bathroom. He then drove out of town, at first heading toward Salt Lake City.

He needed to ditch the car as soon as possible. The police would have the vehicle make and model soon. A few hours into the drive the bandages were soaked. He stopped off at a rest stop to clean the wounds and change the dressing. It was hard to do under the blue public bathroom lights. The blue was supposedly used to deter junkies, making it harder for them to find veins.

When he stepped out of the bathroom, a Mexican was getting out of a beat-to-shit red 4x4 truck. It would do. The Scorpion knifed him right as he was walking by and dumped the Mexican in his trunk. He transferred his gear into the truck as an eighteen-wheeler diesel downshifted and pulled in. Loud Ranchero music blasted over speakers as he started the truck. The Scorpion quickly ejected the CD and tossed it out along the highway as he made a change in direction and took 1-80 West. He drove for several hours before finding a cheap roadside motel with faded manila paint just outside of Reno.

He spent the first few days in his room doped up on Vicodin. By the fourth day, the pain had subsided, and he was able to eat at a nearby diner. His strength returned as soon as he had some solid food in him.

He kept up on the news. The killings were no longer the main story. Nobody cared about a bunch of dead East Europeans with criminal backgrounds. Outside the news, he tried to watch television, but the cable selection was limited. It was mostly newer movies, which he hated. To him, actors and entertainers were pretentious, overpaid dancing monkeys. The Greco Romans had the right idea when they made their entertainers fight it out to the death in Colosseums. He'd pay to watch that.

With nothing grabbing his interest, he stared at the ceiling. He would wait a while longer before he made his next move. He wasn't done with Sin City yet.

Chapter 27

Roddick didn't know what to expect when he first walked into his office. It had been six months since he woke from the dead. Progress was slow. At first, he could hardly speak or move, which had frustrated him because in his head he could do all those things.

The neurologist had told him it looked like all the damage was localized and that he needed to create new pathways to bypass the impaired area. That's what the therapists had tried to do, though at the time he didn't realize it. Playing with play dough while constantly being asked what day it was and who the President of the United States was annoyed him.

It seemed he'd hit a wall as far as progress after the first month. The fear that he would never recover enough to be a fully functional human being briefly came over him. That's when he gave therapy his all, and things picked up.

He managed to stay up longer and put sentences together that didn't sound like gobbledygook to everyone else. He even got to where he could walk long periods without a walker. This allowed him to be discharged. Kaylee stayed with him at the house and took him to his therapy sessions between classes. Eventually, he was able to use public transportation to therapy.

Detective Chase would come by sporadically,

asking about what he remembered. He told him it was the same as the last time he asked. That he went to Valentas and made it look like he had damaging information and that's why he was targeted.

He had planned on ambushing the mysterious killer at the house, and taking him in but it all went to hell. His explanation never seemed to satisfy Chase and he always asked if Roddick could remember more. But there wasn't anything more to remember.

Progress continued to where one would never know he had suffered any type of brain trauma. But to people that knew Roddick, he had changed. He wasn't able to focus for as long as he used to. Nor could he sit through an entire period of hockey before getting bored. This seemed to upset Kaylee, but Shaun and Toney, who would come by, shrugged it off.

Roddick would often leave them to finish the game as he went out for walks to regain his focus. Often he'd go out for hours and when he returned he saw Kaylee had worried he'd gotten lost. Now he kept to shorter walks. Still, he couldn't just walk around all day. He needed to get back to work.

Though his insurance had paid for most of his substantial medical fees, he had dipped into a chunk he had salted away for retirement.

A year earlier, on the suggestion of a client in the banking industry, Roddick had gotten certified as a notary public. It turned out to be fast and easy side money, signing documents and handing them over to the bank. And that's what he planned on doing his first few days. Ease back into things.

For the better part of the morning, he went through the boilerplates for loan signings, property easements, and living trust documents needing to be finalized until the phone rang.

"Vegas Investigations."

There was a disquieting pause at the other end of the line.

"Hello? Can I help you?"

"It's nice to see you're back at work," an ominous voice answered.

"Who is this?"

"You know who it is."

Roddick felt a numbing warmness come over him as his stomach twisted up like a wash cloth being wrung out. His hand tingled as he gripped the phone tighter.

"Why don't we meet up and I can thank you in person for shooting me in the head."

"Your daughter already thanked me for that."

"Right. She told me. Guess I need to take her out shooting some more, seeing as you're still alive."

"She knew what she was doing."

"Is that what you called me about?" Roddick asked.

"No. I called to tell you that the same people that wanted you and your daughter dead are still out there."

"I thought you killed all them in your little rampage at the villa."

"They weren't the ones calling the shots."

"And you want me to help you find out who was?"

"Yes."

"Why the hell should I do that?"

There was another pause. "They will be coming after both of you soon. You can either help me find out who they are or I can do it myself, and when I'm done with them, I will come for you."

The line went dead, and Roddick let the phone slip out of his hand and on to the floor.

****

He stepped off the SDX bus at Casino Center on Carson and into the scorching summer heat. The mercury was already well past a hundred and would only climb higher as the day progressed. The road slithered under the broiling sun like a rattlesnake in search of shade. You never got used to this kind of heat. Not even the locals did.

Roddick was saturated in sweat by the time he stepped into the air conditioned lobby of the Lucky Hearts Casino.

The place had undergone significant upgrades since he had last been there. New slot machines had replaced the acrylic ones, along with new ugly carpet and fixtures. Roddick went and washed the sweat off in the newly remodeled bathroom, half expecting the urinals to be built into a slab of the Berlin Wall like the ones at the Main Street Station Casino.

The staff had been upgraded as well; starting with the new bathroom attendant. At the gaming floor, Roddick did not recognize any of the pit bosses or security personnel. When he showed one of them his card and asked if he could speak with whoever was in charge of the now-revolving door of operations manager, he was told to get lost.

"Just give them my card and tell them I was pals with Jay Lockhart. I'll be on one of them slots over there."

Roddick was on his third spin on the Monopoly Party Train when security found him and grunted something about following them. They went in the back but did not turn to go where Lockhart and Valentas' office had been. They made a left and went up a small stairwell. At the top was an open door and they motioned for him to go in. Roddick wasn't expecting who was on the other side.

A tall, leggy Russian woman with honey-gold hair greeted him. She was dressed in a two-button charcoal jacket and skirt suit, and looked to be in her mid-30s but could easily be in her 40s.

"Hello, I am Tatyana," she said, standing up and extending a friendly hand. "I am head of operations. You are private investigator?"

"Yes."

"I was told you were friends with former operations manager?"

"Yes, seems they've been dropping like flies around here."

"Yes, we've been under a lot of scrutiny because of that. From policemen and media."

"Know anything about it?"

"Only what has been reported in media. They were involved with certain Armenian criminals. Activities that did not involve this casino but brought certain bad attention to it. As you might have gathered, this casino is heavily backed by Russian investors."

"You don't say."

She smiled, and said, "Come." They walked out of the office and along a small balcony that overlooked the gambling pit. "This place was on brink of bankruptcy a few years ago. A group of investors that shall remain nameless came in from Russia and assessed its value. A deal was made."

"Strange that Lockhart never told me about this."

"It was very private matter. What little I'm sure he knew of it he was likely told to keep quiet."

"Why all the secrecy?"

She leaned over the rail and extended her long torso. "Americans get very uptight when foreigners buy American businesses. Why deter possible gamblers and have them go to another casino they think is run by rich Americans?

Roddick tried to hide his scowl. He wasn't buying it.

"Whatever the reason, they certainly made some much-needed upgrades to this place."

"Yes, and business has been doing well, even with bad publicity. Or maybe it turned out to be good thing."

Roddick looked around at the scarce amount of gamblers.

"Yeah, I can see that."

Seeing that he was not buying what she was selling him, she cut the conversation off. "It was very nice speaking with you, Mister Roddick. Please stick around. Gamble."

"You'd like that, wouldn't you?"

She gave him a partial smile and left. He watched her go. It wasn't every day you saw a walking Venus flytrap.

Chapter 28

He wanted coffee, but the closest coffee shop was a hipster joint with wicker chairs and benches with pillows on them. Effeminate men dressed as lumber jacks placed mason jars of coffee in front of patrons who sat playing children's puzzles. The Scorpion wanted them all dead. He stepped up to the counter where a butch-looking lesbian waited for him to order.

"A medium coffee. And I want it in a paper cup."

"Cream and sugar?"

"No."

"And by coffee, I'm assuming you mean the house brew."

"What else would I mean?"

She rolled her eyes and waved toward the menu above her that went the whole scale from lattes to mochas.

"That isn't coffee."

"If you say so."

He paid with a five and waited. He watched as some neckbearded beta male behind him ordered a soy, no foam latte at exactly 195 degrees. The Scorpion wondered if the man had ever had sex with a woman.

When his order arrived, The Scorpion sipped his coffee even though it was still hot out and walked under the lit-up Freemont Street canopy. For almost two months he had been in this area of town, tracking the goings-on of the Lucky Hearts Casino. From shift changes, the staff, what vehicles they drove, and the money drops.

It was fair to say he knew more about the operations of the casino than the people that ran it. Especially the Russian mail-order bride they'd brought in. Though she strutted around like she was born with a tiara up her ass, she was nothing but a prop, and he wanted to know whose casting couch she had to sit on to get the job.

A country band was playing on the 3rd Street Stage near the Four Queens. A nice size crowd cheered them on. The band members were dressed in all the things Johnny Cash despised—eight-gallon hats to rhinestone that went down to their cowboy boots, and belt buckles big enough to fry bacon off of.

Each song they played sounded like the last one. How easy it was to entertain the stupid. Especially the rednecks who made up a good portion of the crowd. No different than the blacks passing by on the crossing streets, blasting out their ooga-booga music.

He kept walking, not moving out of the way of a couple. The man sized him up and saw that it was in his best interests to move. It was a good thing he kept his mouth shut. The Scorpion was in a mood where he'd cut the man's tongue out without hesitation. But he had to control himself. He was still on the police's radar.

That's why he was having Roddick do the digging for him. The Scorpion's investigative work always ended the same way. More dead people meant the police would close in on him faster.

He had to wait.

****

The sun had set, bringing the temperature down to just below a hundred. Roddick was asleep on the deck chair when the sound of Kaylee jumping into the pool stirred him.

"How was the movie with Jessica?" he asked.

"Terrible. It was a boring romance. But it was her pick this time. Pretty sure she was getting me back for making her see horror movies."

"You sure like horror movies."

"I guess I got a thing for psychos," she said as she started to backstroke.

"Yeah, about that. Care to take a guess who called me today?"

Kaylee stopped and shifted upright so that she was bobbing in the water.

"What did he want?"

"Said the people that were after both of us are still around. That it'd only be a matter of time before they come for us again."

"And?"

"And, he wants me to find out who they are."

"So he can kill them."

"I couldn't say…but I'd assume so."

"Have you told the cops?"

"No, not yet. But I did go to the Lucky Hearts Casino. The whole place got an expensive makeover, and they got a real hot Russian lady in charge now."

Kaylee scowled as she hugged the side of the pool in front of him. "Distraction more like it."

"Oh, she's a real honeypot, but not distracting enough to not notice there is some real shady business behind that place. There's enough Russian influence running the casino now that I half expected Vladimir

Putin to walk up and say hello."

"Sounds like you're going to help him."

"I'm not helping that psycho, but I do want to know who wants you and me killed, and why. If there is any chance they are still out there, I'm finding out."

"How can I help?"

"Glad you asked," Roddick said, sitting up in the chair. "I want you to do your tech magic and find out all you can on the casino's finances. How much they're making compared to last year and the year before. And anything else you can find."

"That doesn't sound very exciting."

"It never does at first. But the key to finding out anything in this world is by following the money."

"What are you going to tell the cops?"

"Nothing yet. I tell them, and they'll be all over my ass to help them bring this guy in, which will keep me from finding out who's after us and if they're still a threat."

"Seems you and me both have been keeping a lot from the cops lately," Kaylee said.

"I know. Nothing pissed me off more when I was a cop myself, and people held information back. Yet, here I am."

"I wonder how this ends for him."

"Same way it always ends for people like him. Dead or in prison."

Kaylee nodded, but she wasn't so sure.

Chapter 29

The desk work Roddick had relegated himself to since his return to work was already starting to grow tedious. He may have drawn a line in the sand at not doing domestic cases, but spying on some cheating spouses was starting to sound more appealing. Maybe he could see about getting a workers' comp fraud case. Anything to get the hell out of the office.

Roddick leaned back in his chair and rubbed his temples. Kaylee came in with a can of the liquid nitrogen she drank and a box of donuts from next door.

"When am I going to get a desk?"

"Hell, you can have this one."

She set the donuts on top of a stack of files and took a seat across from him. "Already itching to get out?"

"You're a better detective than I am," he said, grabbing a Boston Cream. "What have you found out?"

"It was hard to get anything definitive. I started with the Nevada Gaming Control Board and took it from there. A rough estimate is the casino made around 16-18 million last year and around 55-70 million in the past six months."

Roddick leaned forward in his chair. "Well, now, that is quite a jump."

"You think the Russians are putting all that money into the place?"

"Not that much. If they were going to invest that heavily they'd have done it for a casino on the Strip. And there's no way they brought in that money from gambling. That place is not even close to being busy enough."

"So has to be other sources of revenue. Drugs?"

"Why buy a casino to sell drugs?"

"A front?"

"Pretty expensive front, wouldn't you say?"

"True."

"We need to talk to an insider, and I know just the guy. Care to take a little father-daughter drive?"

"Thought you'd never ask."

****

The Lakes was a two-mile community centered on Lake Sahara, a man-made lake within city limits. Kaylee zipped her Sonic hatchback along Flamingo Road until it led to a roundabout that put her on Coast Line Court. She drove a short distance until Roddick instructed her to hang a right into a circular driveway that led to a large, single-story stucco house beside the lake.

The house belonged to big-time bookie and Vegas insider Mickey Blundell. Roddick had met him when he was being charged for running illegal gambling lines. His lawyer hired Roddick to do background checks and dig up dirt and find holes with the prosecution's witnesses. It turned out, Roddick got a hold of the original interviewing officer's logs when he first interviewed the state's star witnesses.

The officer wrote side comments such as "untrustworthy" and "manipulative" on his report, which Blundell's lawyer made the officer admit he wrote in court, thus discrediting the witness. The cop was a rookie who made a rookie mistake. It also soured Roddick's reputation with some of the local police.

He pressed the buzzer several times. Blundell answered it dressed in white khakis, a blue polo shirt, aviator glasses, and a sandy mane of hair flowed from his head.

"Jesus, Joe. I heard what happened to you. I'm glad to see you out and about. Come in."

He led them past the large living room out the back to a shaded table on the lake. He waved for them to take a seat and asked Kaylee if she wanted something to drink. She shook her head.

"No, thanks."

"She prefers her energy drinks," Roddick said.

"Kids today," Blundell said. "Cigar?"

"Sure."

He opened a wooden box and handed him a cigar the size of a baby's arm along with a guillotine cutter. Roddick sliced a small chunk off the head and toasted the end so that he got a good puff of smoke.

"Not bad," he said.

They both puffed their stogies for a moment while Kaylee impatiently pulled out her phone. Roddick glanced out on the water at a passing Duffy boat full of drunken tourists. Not far from the boat waterfowl closed in on several floating largemouth bass.

"Lot of dead fish floating out there," Roddick said.

"It happens from time to time. First time it happened, the association brought in the Department of Wildlife. They call it 'turning over,' where I guess there isn't enough oxygen in the lake for all the fish. So a lot of them got to die off until the levels balance out."

A woman on a paddle board screeched as she glided through a group of bellied up fish.

"What happened to you anyway?" Blundell finally asked.

"Got careless. Tried to catch a tiger with a mouse trap. Except at the time, I didn't know it was a tiger."

"He's much worse than a tiger if it's who I think it is."

"What do you know about him, Mickey?"

"Probably as much as you. The Lucky Hearts Casino hired a professional killer to take care of some people that were threatening to expose them. For what, I couldn't say, and I'm sure neither can you, or you wouldn't be here. But this killer they got is as ruthless as they come. They call him The Scorpion. A Nazi motherfucker. Got no problem killing women, kids, little old grandmas, don't matter to him. He wants everyone dead."

"How do you know this?"

"From someone that worked in the same line of business and crossed paths with him once or twice. I say worked because he was suicided. Found him in his hotel room with restraint marks on his hands and a cord to one of the Venetian blinds missing."

Kaylee was no longer on her phone. What Blundell was saying had her full attention.

"What do you think the casino is up to that they'd need someone like this to help cover their tracks?" Roddick asked.

"Could be anything. No secret the whole place is run by the Russian mob. But I honestly have no idea what they're up to. You should talk to Dylan Carter. He's a regular there and seems to win a lot."

"Where's he live?"

"Some shithole studio apartment on Casino Center Boulevard. Though, he might have moved after his recent winning streak."

Roddick thanked Mickey for his time and the cigar and said they'd let themselves out. In the car, Kaylee asked if he wanted to find Dylan.

"Maybe tomorrow," he said. Fatigue was setting in for him. "I think I've had enough fun for one afternoon."

He could barely keep his eyes open on the drive back, so he stopped fighting it and fell asleep against the tinted window.

Chapter 30

The Hideout lived up to its name. An after-hours techno club away from the Strip and hidden in an old converted warehouse. The only way to know when an event was going on was through flyers that were passed along.

It offered a reprieve from the tired top 40s music and recycled DJs the big casinos and Vegas clubs used. It resembled techno clubs in Europe. DJs didn't showboat or wear elaborate costumes but pumped out fast 140-160 beats per minute with no drop.

The Scorpion followed Tatyana to the club and watched as she glided through the crowd to the VIP section, where some man who looked like a cop was waiting for her. The strobe lights and fog machines made it hard for him to get an idea what they were talking about. He found a seat at a small bar away from the acrid odor of the artificial fog and ordered a vodka straight up.

The place was packed with punk girls in leather studded belts and multiple piercings, and men ranging from well-dressed to sleeveless to an assorted few that looked like Nosferatu coming out of a coffin.

An avid observer of non-verbal communications, the Scorpion kept a close eye on Tatyana. From her body language, he could see it was not a flirtatious meeting between her and her male suitor. Most women's faces were animated around people they like while their hands moved to erogenous zones in a sub-conscious effort to draw attention to those areas. Yet Tatyana's face was deadpan while she held her martini glass with both hands the way one would hold a steering wheel of an out of control vehicle.

The man on the other hand, like most ignorant buffoons, was oblivious to these cues and tried to move in closer, not realizing every inch he scooted in, she'd counter by moving a few inches away.

The whole primitive display annoyed the Scorpion. It was like watching monkeys at a zoo. Lab animals, at least, figured out through operative conditioning not to continue to repeat behavior that resulted in getting shocked. If people were hooked up to the same electrodes, their heads would fry.

With no room for her to slide further from him, she stood up and ended the conversation. He didn't follow her but kept an eye on her ass as if someone was going to steal it as she walked out. He smirked, finished his beer, and got up.

The Scorpion stood up and followed him as he cut a path through the crowd of dancers and out the back. There he walked a few blocks and got into a Nissan Maxima with no hub caps.

The Scorpion knew he was a cop.

****

The Studio apartments sat behind a row of palm trees along Casino Center Boulevard. A dull terracotta two-story complex with small carports on the side. A Hispanic housekeeper pushing a cart full of towels and sheets pointed to room 33 when asked where Dylan Carter lived.

Roddick rapped on the door repeatedly.

"He's probably not here," Kaylee said.

"I can hear movement."

The door opened about three inches, enough for a pit bull to stick half its head out and snarl. Kaylee stepped back.

"Jesus Christ," she said.

"He's friendly," a voice behind the door said. A hairy arm reached out and grabbed the spiked collar and pulled the beast back before opening the door the remainder of the way.

The man was middle aged, mid-40s, with a soft belly, thinning brown hair, and thick-framed turtle-shell glasses. He was dressed in shorts, a t-shirt of some heavy metal band, and a Lakers hat.

"You Dylan Carter?" Roddick asked.

"What's it to you?"

"Mickey Blundell said to come see you."

"About what?"

"The Lucky Hearts Casino."

Carter stepped aside and motioned for them to both come in. The apartment was void of almost all furniture except a couple of lawn chairs in the main living area, television and game console, and two large dog bowls. The limited houseware in the sink was old and looked secondhand.

"Excuse the absence of furniture; I don't usually have guests. And since I move around a lot, there's really no point of getting any."

"Why do you move around so much?" Roddick asked.

"Life of a professional gambler. Always moving to the next tournament. Plus, you wear out your welcome fast when you start winning."

"You sure don't look like someone that's been winning."

"Who said I have?"

"Mickey," Roddick said.

"Well, Mickey's got a big mouth it seems."

"Want me to let him know?"

Carter smirked.

"I ain't afraid of Mickey."

"Or the Russian mob apparently."

"That's right."

Roddick looked over at Kaylee, who was petting the dog behind its ears, both of them loving every minute of it.

"You know what? I think you're a liar. Someone who's not afraid doesn't get what looks like a trained pit bull for protection. I bet you just have to give the signal and that harmless pooch right there would rip both our throats out, am I right?"

"There's a lot of break-ins in this area. Nothing wrong with some home protection."

Roddick laughed and waved around the empty apartment. "Yes, because you have so much to protect."

"All right, wise-ass, why don't you take your underage whore and get the fuck out."

"I'm his daughter, you pig," Kaylee yelled.

"Sure you are, sweetie," he said.

Roddick leaned in fast and grabbed Carter's nose between his fingers and started to twist. The dog perked up, waiting for the command to lunge.

"You send that thing at me, and I'll rip your goddamn nose off and shove it down its throat."

"All right, all right. Let go, dammit!"

Roddick released his grip and Carter moved back. He rubbed his nose and looked to see if there was blood.

"I think you broke it!" he whined.

"Shut up, it's fine. How much money have you won at the Lucky Hearts Casino?"

"I dunno. Half a mil, I think."

"How do you not know for sure if you won half a million from a casino?"

"I dunno, I blow it as fast as I win it."

"So, it's all gone?"

He didn't answer.

"Where's the money, Carter?"

"Yes, it's all gone."

Roddick rubbed his temples. The conversation was tiring him. Carter was a stupid little man who wasn't being honest with him. He could spend all afternoon pressing him and get little in return. He stood up, pulled out one of his cards and handed it to him.

"In case you smarten up and want to tell me the truth before it's too late."

Carter studied the card as if it was written in another language.

"Yeah, sure. I'll do that," he said and slipped it into his pocket.

Roddick and Kaylee headed to the door but not before the dog trotted to Kaylee for one last scratch behind the ears

"He's lying," Kaylee said, once they were back in the car on their way home.

"I know. He's scared to death."

They didn't say anything but were thinking of the same person.

Chapter 31

Things were looking up for Chase. The fatal shooting of an overnight bank security guard led McCartney and him tracking down a stolen forklift used to rip out an ATM machine.

They found the forklift in an old industrial warehouse on West Desert Inn. The forklift wasn't the only thing they found, though. It turned out to be the motherload of stolen merchandise. Ranging from cars, neon street signs, slot machines, and the ATM still intact. The owner and his pal both claimed ignorance but ratted each other out under heavy questioning at the station.

Chase was still looking into his boogeyman contract killer, but only in his spare time. He had gotten a hold of Keesey and some of the dead Armenian's phone records and thoroughly combed through them. Most of the numbers ended up being dead ends. There were a few text messages, and most of the providers they had did not keep the contents of the messages.

One of the numbers on Keesey's phone belonged to a stripper, Scarlett Hewitt, who was also one of the deceased at the villa massacre. Chase went to the club she worked at, The Lusty Lady, and some of the girls said they knew her and recognized a photo of Keesey. Said he was a regular, but that was all they could remember.

144

The thing Chase kept going back to was the young brunette his hitman was seen with at the Sandman Motel. He had gone back and questioned all the staff, and one of the maids said she saw her leaving the room once or twice. Described her as having freckles and said that her hair did not look like her natural color.

"Why would he stay in a motel with this young girl?" Chase mumbled out loud.

McCarthy looked up from his own paperwork. He knew what Chase was talking about because he had been obsessing over the case for months.

"I told you. She was probably some whore he got."

"Right, because he's going to shoot up a motel full of Armenian thugs just to rescue some whore?"

"These psychos get possessive of what they see as their property."

Chase shook his head.

"Not this guy. He gives no fucks about anyone. He either needed her for something, or she caught his interest somehow. Probably both."

"You need to let this one go. He's gone."

"For now. But I don't think we've seen the last of his destruction."

****

The GPS showed the Nissan Maxima moving. The Scorpion had managed to catch up to the unmarked police car as it was leaving the club and followed it until it made a stop at a 24-hour discount liquor store on Spring Mountain Road.

The cop stayed in the store long enough for the Scorpion to slip the tracker under the chassis. He was now keeping tabs on it along with Tatyana and a few others from his GPS display as he sat in a parked black

Chevy Impala SS.

It was the early morning hours, yet the police radio was blurting out reported gunshots and a possible homicide at an apartment on Casino Center Boulevard. He re-checked the GPS again. The Nissan Maxima was en route there. The Scorpion started the Impala's powerful V8 engine and pulled away from the curb. He was going to see what it was all about.

****

An early morning crowd of commuters and onlookers were assembled out front of the Studio. Responding officers were fast on rolling out the barricade tape and keeping everyone back. Chase and McCartney got out of the car and went up to where all the action was.

Room 33 was wide open with an officer standing guard. They walked in, and the first thing Chase zeroed in on was that there was hardly any furniture. A robbery? It was too fast a response time to steal large furniture. In the middle of the studio, a middle-aged man in nothing but drawstring shorts lay face down with a right size hole in his cranium. Near him was a Glock 9mm next to a couple patio chairs and two dog bowls. Where was the dog?

As if reading his mind, one of the officers first on the scene said, "Neighbor next door said she heard a gunshot followed by screaming and loud barking. She said the guy that lives here owned a pit bull named Chopper."

"Where's Chopper now?" McCarthy asked.

"I don't know. The door was open when we arrived, so he must have taken off."

The forensic investigator from the coroner's office

stepped in as Chase observed the scene.

"Bag the gun after you finish the cataloguing," Chase said. "Chances are it'll be unregistered. Another kit model."

"Sounds like our hitman is back," McCarthy said.

Chase looked at the sizable amount of blood that went out of the apartment. "Don't think so. Looks like Chopper bit a good chunk off our killer. No way would our guy do this type of job not knowing his target had a man-eating dog for protection. Whoever did this, wanted us to think it was him."

"Why would they go through all that trouble?"

"I don't think it was supposed to be that much trouble. They just didn't account for the dog."

Chase noticed a white card on the floor, almost against the edge of the wall. He walked over to it, careful to avoid any blood. Staring down at it, without moving it, he saw Roddick's name.

"Interesting," he said and pulled out his phone. An hour later Roddick and Kaylee showed up.

"Thanks for coming," Chase said as he walked over to them.

"No problem. Besides, I kind of had a feeling I'd be back here in this type of manner."

"Why do you say that?"

"When we talked with him the other day, he looked like a marked man. Jesus, there's a lot of blood. And where's that dog of his?"

"Ran off but not before attacking the suspect. We got officers and animal control out looking for the dog now."

"Are you going to put him down?" Kaylee asked.

"That I don't know. We just want to get the animal

before it harms anyone."

"Forget about the damn dog," Roddick said. "You need to go after the Lucky Hearts Casino. Pretty much anyone that is connected to them that I've spoken with has ended up dead."

"What was Mr. Carter's connection to the casino," McCarthy asked.

"He had won a lot of money from them recently. It didn't seem legit. Wanted to question him about it but he wasn't exactly forthcoming. Why I left my card on the off chance he wanted to tell me the truth. But as you can see, that ain't going to happen."

"My partner thinks it was the same guy that attacked you that did the job," Chase said.

"If it were him, he'd have known about the dog and killed it first," Kaylee said.

The comment got Chase's attention. The certainty of it, as if she had personal dealings with him. He looked at her and saw a young woman with similar features to her father minus the red hair and freckles.

"Freckles," Chase mumbled.

"Excuse me?" Roddick asked.

"Nothing. Thanks again for coming and answering our questions. I'll keep in touch."

Chapter 32

He was parked a reasonable distance away but saw everything through a pair of 7x50 tactical binoculars. The Scorpion watched as the two plainclothes cops got out of the Nissan Maxima and went up to the apartment.

Almost an hour later two men pushing a gurney with a body bag on it slid the stiff in the back of a white Ford SUV that read *Clark County Coroner* with the number 14183 just below the driver's side mirror.

Kaylee's blue Chevy Sonic pulled up not long after that. The Scorpion gripped the wheel hard as he saw her get out of the car. Part of him wanted to shoot her dead right then and there, but the other part still held a fascination. Flashes of her naked shadow against the shower curtain came over him, and he let go of the wheel.

He didn't follow when Roddick and Kaylee got back in the car and left several minutes later. He lolled for an hour after until the two cops got back into their machine. He let them drive off as he switched from his binoculars to the GPS display. They were headed back to Cheyenne Avenue. A busy afternoon full of paperwork and donuts. *Fucking pigs.*

He checked the time. It was nearing noon. He would get something to eat and then find out what the hell this was all about.

****

Chase had finished writing up the last of the witness reports when McCarthy came back. "Found Chopper. He attacked a Jehovah Witness a few blocks away while she was getting out of her car. Then he started ripping the bumper off the arriving squad car. Animal Control was able to get him with one of them restraining poles."

"Christ," Chase said. "Is the woman okay?"

"Oh, yeah. Taking her to the hospital now. Animal Control said the dog's got one of them rabies vaccination tags, so I guess she won't need rabies shots."

"I suppose it could have been a lot worse."

"Hell yeah, it could've been. Like that kid that got mauled by one of them things a few months back."

"Yes, I remember. They had him in the hospital for months trying to reconstruct his face… Hey, speaking of hospitals, can you go see if anyone has been treated for dog bites in the last few days. It's a long shot, but we might get lucky."

"On it."

Soon as McCarthy left, Chase turned to his computer and put in Kaylee Roddick. No priors, DMV records showed a speeding ticket in Rhode Island; seventy-five in a fifty-five. Went to traffic school to get it reduced. Current insurance policy. Everything on the surface looked clean. The maid at the Sandman Motel said the brown hair didn't look like the girl's natural hair color. Red hair would stand out. If she wanted to be less noticeable, she'd have to wear some sort of wig.

Chase sighed. It was a good bet his suspicions would lead to nothing. But he had to rule them out.

That was what good police work was. Or so he told himself.

****

The call Roddick was expecting at his office came a little past ten in the morning. When he answered there was the usual long pause before the caller demanded, "What have you found out?"

"No small talk with you, is there?"

No answer

"Fine. Since the Russians have taken over the place, the casino has tripled their total yearly profits in the last six months. Which means—"

"The money is coming from somewhere else."

"Exactly. Not only that but a person who happened to have won big at the casino and who I recently spoke with, is now dead."

"Yeah, I know."

"Do you know this because you happened to be the one responsible?"

Another long pause. "I'm starting to wonder if I over-estimated your abilities."

"I know it wasn't you. But they're trying to make it look like it was you. Leaving the same type of unmarked gun at the scene."

"It's simple. They think they can draw the attention away from them and pin everything on me. As far as they know, I'm no longer in Vegas."

"What's your next move?" Roddick asked.

"What makes you think I have one?"

"Are you kidding? Between them long pauses I can hear your brain clicking. You're calculating something."

"It's none of your concern at this point."

"If it's going to put my daughter and me in danger I'd say it is."

Another pause.

"I'm going to find out where the money is coming from."

"How?"

There was no answer. Only the sound of a line ending.

****

Half an hour after being hung-up on, Roddick stepped off the 206 bus on Freemont Street. He had traced the call number to a pay phone below a vintage sign that read Par-A-Dice Motel with a pair of red dice next to the name just to make sure people got the name. The motel had long been demolished, but the sign still remained. A reminder perhaps of Vegas old. Even the pay phone itself was a relic of a bygone era. Though, there was still a good amount of them left in the city, used mostly for shady reasons.

Roddick looked around. He wasn't far from the Lucky Hearts Casino. That wasn't a coincidence. He figured the Scorpion was staying close to the casino. Doing some sort of recon no doubt. Planning his next attack. How many people would he kill this time?

The mid-afternoon heat was starting to get to him as he kept walking down Freemont toward the casino. His therapist had warned him of over-exerting himself. But he'd never cared for the kid-glove treatment. He had to push through it like he did with all things in his life. That was why he wasn't a cop anymore. There was no room in these over-politically-correct times for cops doing what needed to be done. Christ, seemed like you couldn't even do a routine traffic stop anymore without getting accused of being some kind of racist.

The mist from a restaurant patio felt good as it sprayed over Roddick when he passed by, bringing his temperature down a notch. The casino's air conditioning felt even better as he walked in and went straight to the bar. He mopped the sweat off his face with his shirt that was soaked through. The beer he got was even nicer. He found a comfortable chair nearby and was resigned to never get up from it.

He sipped his beer and watched as all walks of humanity came in and out. Elderly people that belonged in a nursing home, not in front of a slot machine all day, and human trash of every variety. The few rich-looking people were not there to gamble. They were East Europeans in expensive suits that paid no attention to the slots or tables or even the attractive hostesses. All business. Drug traffickers more than likely.

A familiar leggy blonde greeted the men. Tatyana. They spoke for several minutes and left. She turned on her heel as if on a carousel and that's when she saw him. He finished the rest of his beer and stood up as she approached.

"Mister Roddick, what brings you by?"

"Honestly, the air conditioning."

"Yes, it is quite cold in here. I've had enough cold for a lifetime. I would much rather be out enjoying the heat."

"It'll get old after a while. Trust me."

"That I doubt."

"Who were your friends? They looked pretty serious."

She was about to say something but held back. "Clients, if you must know."

"They didn't seem all that interested in gambling."

"They are not those type of clients."

"Of course not."

"You seem to be implying something," she said.

"Let's just cut the bull. I know this casino is some sort of front. So why don't you just tell me what sort of operation you're really running here."

"You act like I'm under some obligation to do so. Is there something I should know, Mister Roddick?"

"Yes, the hired killer your casino brought in. You know, the one that killed the two guys that held your job and put a bullet in my head. The one you are trying to pin Dylan Carter's murder on. He's here."

Her eyes flickered, but she hid her fear well. "You have spoken with this man?"

"More or less."

"What does he want?"

"The hell if I know. But seeing how he handles things, I'd say he wants you and who else is running things dead."

She laughed. "You should save your skills for the poker tables, Mister Roddick."

"Oh, this isn't a bluff, beautiful. This honestly is your last chance to wise up and tell me what's going on."

"And you will protect me? You can't even protect yourself from him."

"You are right, but the police can put you into protective custody."

"I already have policeman for protection. Several in fact."

Roddick stepped back.

"Who?"

She smiled.

"I was wrong. You are not so good poker player."

She turned and left him standing in the lobby.

Chapter 33

Police emergency lights were flashing as Detective Chase pulled into the parking lot of the Sandman Motel. They were easy to miss at first, for it was around the time of day where the last moments of natural sunlight transitioned into bright, exaggerated lights built on rocket ship dreams. A 1950s style Space Age wonderland where the popping slot machine displays and exaggerated cursive street signs made something like police lights pale in comparison.

A familiar detective along with a uniformed officer was at the reception area. The detective, Craig Morgan, was a tall, heavy-set, well-liked senior officer. His egg-shaped belly, from the years of stress and no time to eat anything but fast food, had long crested over his belt line. A gray curly cop-stache and thick dark eyebrows were about all the hair he had left.

"What's all the excitement here?" Chase asked Morgan, after shaking hands and exchanging pleasantries.

"Suicide. Cleaning lady found one of the guests hanging like a wind chime in his shower. A Grady Hamilton, forty-seven-year-old male out of Santa Rosa."

"He leave a note?"

"Yeah, in his briefcase. The usual crap. Recently divorced. Laid off. Battling depression, yada, yada."

"Any signs they tried to move the body to somewhere else?"

Hotel/Motels in Vegas sometimes moved bodies to avoid keeping the room from being quarantined and costing them money.

"Not that I could tell. He was still hanging in the shower stall when we arrived. Didn't look like the room was disturbed much."

Chase nodded.

"What brings you here?"

"Here to talk to one of the maids. See if I can get a positive ID on someone."

"Busy night, wouldn't you say?" Morgan said to the young female receptionist. She smiled.

"Not the kind of busy we like."

" 'Course not. We'll be out of your hair as soon as we can."

"Is Beverly Sanchez in?" Chase asked the receptionist.

"Bev? She should be around still. She's, um…the one that found Mr. Hamilton."

Chase located Ms. Sanchez smoking by the pool. She was middle-aged, still reasonably attractive, with ash-blondish hair and dark brown skin.

"I would like to just go one month without finding someone dead in their room," she said as he approached.

Vegas tried to keep secret the real number of people who died in their room from natural causes, suicides, drugs, or murder. The press hardly ever reported it. They didn't want to get on the bad side of the hotel/casino businesses.

"I don't blame you," Chase said.

157

He sat across from her on one of the poolside lounge chairs and dabbed some of the sweat off his face. Though the sun had long disappeared, the heat remained.

"Last month at another hotel I work at, I come in to change the bedsheet, and some guy is lying chained to the damn bed with a needle sticking out of him. And that's not even the worst of it. It was all the sex toys he had around. Looked like a medieval torture dungeon. It's bad enough I'm trying to raise two kids in this perverted town, but I have to walk into stuff like that."

"I hear you. I always wondered how anyone could raise a family here and yet people do. And they seem to turn out okay, I suppose."

"You have to have a faith. Churches here keep a lot of families and their kids from straying."

She's probably right. Would explain why Vegas had one of the highest numbers of churches per capita.

He pulled out and unfolded a piece of printer paper. It was a blown-up photo of Kaylee's driver's license.

"The young girl you saw that you said might not be a real brunette. Did she look like this?"

She took the paper and studied it for a moment.

"Perhaps. I only got brief glimpses of her. But yes, it could certainly have been her."

Chase stuffed the paper back in his pocket.

"What about the man she was with. Any more details about him come to mind?"

"No. He was very non-distinct. Except for the short spiky hair. I'd seen it before with military men."

"What else?"

"I don't know what else I can tell you. Except how

I felt the one time he passed by me. I felt uneasy to the point I stepped back into the room I was attending."

"He made you that uncomfortable?"

"I can sense things from people. You can laugh all you want. But I can. And that man put out a very dark presence."

****

Carl followed Tatyana as she stepped into a private cabin on the High Roller observation wheel. The Lucky Heart Casino, who he did business with, required that his company do 24/7 protection on her and that he handle it personally. That told Carl she must be pretty important. So he had been accompanying her for the past week.

If she wasn't working at the Casino she was shopping or sunbathing. She told him the heat felt good compared to where she was from. Between slathering suntan lotion on every fifteen minutes by the pool, she talked of the brutal winters in St. Petersburg where she had spent most of her life. How she would go months without sun.

He didn't mind listening to her. She was nice to look at in a bikini. He could tell she was used to people gawking at her. She told him modeling agencies had been after her since she was thirteen, but she had no interest in that.

"Why model when you could be the one making money from the models?"

"That's a good point," he told her.

"Most of my simple-minded friends went and got married and had kids. Me, I got a degree in management and worked consultant and bank management jobs. And now, here I am, in charge of a casino."

Carl now watched her as she rolled out her yoga mat and placed headphones on. She told him she had reserved the private, silent yoga session weeks out before there was finally an opening. Carl never understood the popularity of yoga. Especially with women. Bending your limbs in positions they weren't meant to go.

He could hear, through her headphones, a voice directing her to let go of worldly possessions as the cabin started to rise above the slot machines, shops, and material temptations.

He watched as she concentrated on her breathing and he tried to do the same. But there was too much on his mind to stay in the present moment. She told him the reason she needed protection was because a private detective named Roddick came by the casino and warned her that some psychotic hitman was back in town.

The same one that killed the person whose position she took over. He'd heard rumblings about this hitman and how he was anything but incompetent at what he did. If he was after her, that would make his job very difficult. The last thing he needed was one of his clients getting killed.

The cabin reached the height of its ascent at 550 feet above the city. It was clear enough outside that Carl could see the reddish colors from Red Rock Canyon. They went around for a second rotation as Tatyana moved into sun salutations. He could see why she wanted a cabin to herself. Being as tall and as long-limbed as she was, she needed the room to fully extend. Being a bigger guy himself, he could relate.

"Tell me, Carl," she said as they stepped out of the cabin and started down the platform "Suppose he shows up right now, how would you handle him?"

"With ease, Ma'am. I've had lots of training."

"The policeman I spoke with told me you were in military before starting up your protection business."

"That's right."

"Have you killed many people?"

"Not as a civilian but yes, when I was in Iraq and Afghanistan."

"When I was child, I remember my parents complaining how it seemed like our country would never get out of Afghanistan. Now it's same for you Americans, yes?"

"Yes, Ma'am. I don't see a real exit plan of ever getting out of that God-forsaken land."

"It took the fall of the Soviet Union for my country to get out."

"There's always a price for this kind of war," Carl said.

"Yes, there is."

Chapter 34

It was sweltering hot as Kaylee crossed the pedestrian bridge above Las Vegas Boulevard toward the city library.

The structure looked like something out of a Geometry textbook. Near the entrance, a cone structure made to look like a party-hat held birthday parties. Next to it, a concrete 112-foot- tall gray science tower in the shape of an empty toilet paper roll overlooked the city. It was all made from native sandstone and concrete to help deflect the brutal summer heat, which Kaylee was escaping from.

She had been searching heavily into unsolved murders similar to the Scorpion's method. She learned that he often left an unregistered Glock at the scene and also looked for witnesses who described seeing someone that fit his description.

She got a few hits and used several search engine newspaper archives to gather more information. Most of the hits failed the vetting process. Either the suspect didn't fit the Scorpion's appearance, or there was too little information to go on.

Her last option was to see if there were any hard copies from the libraries vast microfiche catalog of newspaper articles. She found several papers, with the desired dates, and sat in front of the microfiche reader. It was a tedious process, but slowly she scratched each promising lead off except one from seven years earlier.

Arthur Cook, 45, found dead in a burning trash can. In the 300 block of Brighton Park, March 25. Gunshot wound to the back of the head. Unregistered Glock 9mm was recovered in the trash can. Hands were bound. Believed Cook was shot execution style, stuffed in the trash can and set on fire. One eyewitness said she saw a man of average height and build with short blondish spiky hair in the area shortly before the fire was reported.

Kaylee found Cook's obituary in the following paper. He was an advertisement executive out of Chicago. Married with two daughters, Andrea and Rachel, around her age. His wife, Katherine, committed suicide a few years later. No doubt from grief and anger over the killer never being found.

From comments Kaylee found from the oldest daughter Andrea's public postings on her social media sites, her dad had a drug problem. More specifically, cocaine. Andrea had told a friend she was pretty convinced he owed some drug dealers a lot of money and that's how he ended up the way he did. Jeez. The things people posted.

Even so, a sinking feeling came over Kaylee. She knew she hadn't even scratched the surface of the horrors the Scorpion had done. Because of him, those two girls no longer had parents. She should have shot him in the head when she had the opportunity. She had caught him with his guard down, but she knew he would not make that mistake again.

****

The afternoon sun punished the wasteland an hour from Vegas. Heat waves zig-zagged and forked out across the endless barren stretch of sand, limestone, and various forms of desert flora and cacti.

There was little life to be seen except for the Scorpion, who seemed unaffected by the heat as he walked across the scorching landscape. He parked the Impala off Mercury Highway near where Camp Desert Rock used to be and started walking.

In the distance, a brown and black streaked roadrunner banged a kangaroo rat repeatedly against a rock before sprinting across the aridisol terrain toward a thicket of scrub brush. The Scorpion kept walking. He had spent his idle time building pipe bombs. This time opting to make them out of metal water piping instead of PVC pipe like the previous ones. He cut them in half inch lengths and filled them full of gunpowder, glass, and nails before capping them off. Now he needed to test them to see if the pressure was right and he couldn't think of a more fitting area than where they used to test atomic bombs.

Further in, he came across an abandoned military airfield with a sole northeast/southeast strip with a nearby white and orange windsock that dropped from the pole it hung off of from lack of wind.

He kept moving along the five thousand feet of cracked and potted runway until he found a hidden enough spot and took out one of the bombs from his pack. He stuck it in a small hill of sand and ignited the fuse. He walked away casually until he was a safe enough distance to watch as the flame inched down into the hole he had drilled for the fuse.

The hill erupted and sent a plume of sand into the air. The casing had proven to be strong enough that it had built up a significant amount of pressure. But what the Scorpion was most interested in was the amount of damage. He walked the circumference of the blast area and spotted chunks of steel piping and nails. Anyone close to the bomb was going to get shredded.

The Scorpion smiled.

He tested out a few more bombs. All produced similar results. There would be no loose ends this time. He was going to kill anyone that was any kind of importance at the Lucky Hearts Casino. He no longer cared about the rest of the money owed to him. He wanted to make sure that the insects he took jobs from never got the idea they were equal to him, and that they had better think twice about double-crossing someone who was that much more superior to them.

To him, he was no different than the fireball and mushroom clouds that once lit the Nevada sky. And like him, the shockwave and nuclear fallout that came with such bombs did not care who it killed or maimed. The sick, the elderly, women, children, priests, good Samaritans, it didn't matter; they all suffered the same judgment of irrelevancy when faced against a superior power.

****

The nuts and bolts of detective work was interviewing people and following up on every new piece of information no matter how tedious it was. It was a daily grind and a frustrating one when you didn't get the results you wanted. Yet there was nothing like getting that big break you were looking for. That's what Detective Chase got when looking at Dylan Carter's financial records.

Carter had been flagged dozens of times for suspicious activity. Several casinos had reported currency transactions Carter had made with the Treasury Department Financial Crimes Enforcement Network for deposits and withdrawals upward of ten to twenty thousand dollars at a time. W-2G forms he filed showed he had "won" over a million dollars at various casinos. The most being at the Lucky Hearts.

Normally these types of currency transaction reports were not a big deal in a gambling capital like Vegas. But with all the murder going around linked to the Lucky Hearts Casino, things were stacking up.

"He was doing money laundering," Chase told McCarthy as he took a seat at his desk across from him.

"Who, Carter? Hell, ain't that obvious? Still don't tell us who killed him."

"We need to put the pressure on the Lucky Hearts."

"Yeah, well, good luck with that. No judge will sign any kind of warrant to do anything against a casino without a full-on confession from the casino owners themselves."

It was true. That was what happened when you had the Clark County Courthouse sitting only a few blocks away from casinos, strip clubs, and drive-thru wedding chapels. Judges shamelessly awarded large sums of money in judgments to people they didn't even hide being associated with, more specifically in the form of casinos and large law firms.

"You're right," Chase said. "We need to get a confession."

"From who? So far the only witness we got to Carter's murder is that man-eating pit bull, and they already euthanized him."

Chase hadn't told McCarthy yet about his suspicions with Kaylee possibly being the girl that was with their hitman. He needed more to go on. But if it did turn out to be her, she was the one that could blow the lid off it all.

"I wasn't talking about the dog. Something else I'm working on."

Chase was relieved that McCarthy didn't even bother to ask him to elaborate. They'd worked with each other long enough to know when it was best to just let their partner work out whatever the hell was going on in his head

Chase turned his attention to the composite sketch he had tacked up behind his desk. It was supposedly what his hired killer looked like according to the server at Ralph's Diner. Chase had his doubts on how reliable the sketch was. For one, if you put it next to the composite done of the Zodiac killer, minus the glasses they'd be almost identical. So much so some of the other detectives had fun with it by tacking on post-it notes with cryptograms to solve.

"Is this guy that good or that lucky?" Chase asked.

"Probably both."

"I used to think that if you did good detective work, asked the right questions, looked at every possibility, every shred of evidence, you'd almost always get your man. And that's been true for the most part. But with this one…feels like we're stuck in some kind of real life Mobius strip. We're just going around and around as bodies keep stacking up, and every time we seem to be making headway, it goes nowhere."

"He'll slip up. And it will be over the most mundane thing like a burned-out taillight at a routine traffic stop."

Chase nodded. McCarthy was right. People behind

some of the biggest crimes got caught that way. Hopefully, history would repeat itself. Chase needed it to.

****

The Scorpion's black Impala was an earthy reddish-yellow from the desert dust and in need of a wash when he pulled it into the *Fabulous Mr. Washman* off West Anne Road. The waiting area was clean, with the AC keeping it cool enough to house blocks of ice.

The Scorpion opted to stand over sitting in the lounge chairs and watch through the window as the neon sign switched from pre-wash to washing to waxing. He strolled through the small gift shop with greeting cards and toys, and stopped at a hanging rubber mask of Elvis with his classic combed back pompadour and sideburns. The molding of his features hadn't set right and looked like a poorly done embalming procedure.

He purchased it along with a pack of chewing gum and walked out to the freshly washed vehicle. One of the employees was finishing drying it by hand and stood waiting for an appraisal of his work and a tip. The Scorpion gave him neither, as he got in and drove out.

He kept driving until he found a dive bar on a side street off Flamingo, just behind the Strip. The sign was offering quarter-pound all-beef hotdog and a bottle of domestic beer for $2.50. Hungry, he parked and went in. Just inside the door to the right was a convenience store supplied with everything you'd expect. He kept going to one of the bars near the main entrance and ordered a beer and dog while he took in his surroundings.

From the crowd, the place was a mecca of

debauchery. A transvestite sat at one of the many slot machines, smoking a fresh cigarette while two smoldering ones sat in the nearby ashtray. A one-legged man, with a naked woman carved into the handle of his wooden cane, chatted with a strung-out younger woman about which drinks they preferred.

The half-clothed female bartender came back with his order. She wore tight, low-riding pants, where the straps of her underwear were exposed, and a top that cut off at about her armpits. She had her long black hair tied in a ponytail, and one eye green and the other swollen.

"You didn't do a good enough job concealing that black eye your husband gave you," he said.

She bit her lips with surprise. "What was that?"

Ignoring her, he went on. "There's no point in concealing it if the swelling hasn't gone down. Something like a frozen silver dollar on your eye would've done the trick."

He watched as she first looked stunned at his comment, then leaned over the bar, clearly hoping to distract him long enough with her ample cleavage. . He didn't pay attention to the show, but kept burning a hole right through her.

"It's not like that. I tripped."

He finished his beer and placed the bottle on the counter.

"It's not a good habit to lie to people when you're not especially good at it."

"Just who the hell are you and how did you know I was married??"

As if bored, the Scorpion said, "You got slight discoloration on your ring finger, meaning you just recently took it off."

"How observant of you. I take it off when I'm working. I get better tips when the pervs think I'm single."

"You can keep the ring off permanently," he said.

"What do you mean?"

"I can take care of your husband for you if you want me to."

She stepped back. "Of course not. He didn't mean…"

"So, you're fine with what he's doing to you?"

"No. I didn't say that. Just who the hell are you?"

"Someone in the business of getting rid of people."

Unable to look away from him, she could tell he wasn't joking. A mixture of fear and excitement rushed through her eyes.

"How much?"

"How much do you got?"

"I got a thousand put away but could sell off some stuff, maybe two thousand."

The Scorpion stood up and dropped what spare change he had left on the counter.

"If I were you, I'd take that money and get a divorce attorney."

He walked out, pleased at how fast he was able to get a random stranger willing to pay him to kill someone.

Chapter 35

The thunder was loud as The Scorpion sat quietly in a moonstone comfort chair. He could hear her moving from inside her bedroom. He waited. It was a nice place. The floor to ceiling windows of the condo showed almost all the cityscape. He could see her marveling at the view. But there would be no marveling tonight. The thunder continued to echo off in the distance. The bedroom door opened and he watched as Tatyana stepped out fully nude and slowly walked toward him.

Fear flickered in her large blue eyes as she scanned him. He watched her spot the pair of legs sticking out from behind her Ottoman.

"So much for high-priced security," she said.

"He never had a chance."

The Scorpion's reply unsettled her but not as much as his disinterest in the fact she wasn't wearing anything. The womanly assets that had served her all her life meant nothing to him. Instead, he looked straight through her like she didn't even exist. Her hands twitched. She turned and grabbed a cigarette off the marble kitchen counter and lit it. He didn't move.

"So you are the one that has been giving us so much trouble."

He didn't answer.

"Are you here to kill me?"

"You already know the answer to that," he said.

"Why haven't you done so already?"

"Because you are going to tell me everything I want to know."

She laughed. "Or else you will torture me?"

The Scorpion let his silence answer the question.

"In Russia, I'd grown accustomed to the possibility of being tortured. My uncle was once picked up off the street by the FSB and had electrodes attached to him. They cranked the current up so he would be made to "dance" from all the convulsions. So you see, it is a way of life. But here in America, I find most people don't have the stomach for such things. Yet you probably find great pleasure in inflicting as much pain as possible on others."

"What pleasure I once found in doing such a thing has long past. It is only a means to get what I need."

Tatyana saw the black canvas bag by his feet He could see she was trying hard not to tremble or show fear. He watched as she looked at her cigarette and saw that it burnt down to the filter. She smashed it out on the countertop ashtray and opened her purse next to it. He didn't move. Not even when she pulled out a Sig P238, stuck it in her mouth and fired.

She fell to the ground and twitched for a few seconds. The Scorpion watched as all sign of life drained out of her. A few moments later he took the Glock he had hidden just beside him and stuck it in his pocket as he stood up. His face twitched with annoyance. Cowards. All of them. He grabbed the canvas bag and let himself out.

****

He stepped out of the shower and still smelled like

her signature fragrance from some expensive Himalayan flower no doubt. Toney sprayed himself down with his own body spray to try and get it off, then wrapped a cotton towel around his waist.

Mikaela was now on his bed having slipped back into her underwear.

It was hard to believe he was sleeping with an up-and-coming pop star but sometimes these things happened. Mikaela was booked solid at the casino for the next month, and Carl had put him in charge of her security detail.

He had no idea who she was. But that was no knock against her; he'd lost touch with popular music decades ago. His knowledge of music ended with classic rock and hair bands.

From the start, she'd proven to be one of the more difficult celebrities he dealt with. For starters, her tour rider was ridiculous. It was pages of demands such as the temperature had to be exactly 72 degrees at all times, along with cases of bottled water, freeze-dried fruit, specific beverages, candles, fresh flowers, in particular Hollyhill black dahlias, along with directions that drivers, security, and stage crew were not allowed to talk or look at her unless directed otherwise.

He personally handled her security for the first few shows of her lip-synching through the entire set list. She must have seen the displeasure on his face because she demanded he tell her what he thought of her performance. He was fast to tell her that there was so much autotune going on it sounded like robots fucking. He was counting on the crack getting him kicked off her security detail, but instead, she demanded he be there for all her shows.

His first thought was that she did this to torment him, but one night after the show she made him carry her to her dressing room because she claimed she was too tired to walk. They ended up drinking a lot of champagne and bumping uglies in her penthouse bed.

She was beautiful, to say the least, with long, curly brown hair, olive skin, and plump red lips. He wasn't so bad looking himself and was still in fantastic shape for his age. Whether she was having some Neo-Freudian Electra Complex with him, he couldn't say nor did he care.

She looked up from her phone when she saw him slipping into a fresh pair of boxer shorts.

"You going to take me back to my room, tiger?"

"You can't wait until morning?"

"No, I'm meeting some people from some magazine I don't even remember the name of."

A phone rang. From the ringtone, Toney knew it was his. He looked around for the pants he had been wearing, found them under the bed, and forged through the pockets for the phone before the call went to voicemail. He grabbed it in time to see that it was Carl.

"I need you to check on Jarvis. He's watching over Tatyana. I've been trying to get a hold of him for a status check, but he isn't answering."

Carl, for the most part, was a very easy going boss but he had one major rule. Constant communication while on the job. For someone not to respond back, meant something was up.

"I'd do it myself," he stated. "But I'm stuck with this MMA fighter who wants to do an all-nighter with his posse. I'm telling you now, put money down on his opponent. This guy isn't taking his shit seriously."

Toney laughed. "Yeah, I was heading out anyways. I'll go see what's going on."

"When you do see Jarvis, tell him to call me immediately."

Toney said he would and ended the call. By the sound of Carl's voice, he'd hate to be Jarvis right now.

****

Mikaela kept flipping through the stations in his truck until she found some pop station. Toney groaned as he accelerated the Hemi V8 in the direction of the MGM Grand.

"Trying to get rid of me," she joked.

"No. Just got something I got to check on for work."

"Another woman you're babysitting, perhaps? Do I know her?"

"Don't be stupid."

"What would you do if I told the people from the magazine tomorrow that I'm sleeping with my bodyguard?"

Toney turned to look at her quickly, squinting his eyes, praying she was joking. The sound of Carl's disgruntled voice when he'd told him to have Jarvis call him echoed in his ear. Toney could only imagine the anger if Carl found out he was fucking one of his top clients.

She laughed. "You should see your face. I should seriously take a picture."

"Bitch," he cursed as he steered the massive truck to the front of the casino.

She looked out the tinted window to make sure nobody was watching, then leaned over, whispering into his ear, "Best not forget. I own your ass." She stepped out and strutted away.

"What the hell did I get myself into?" he muttered as he pulled out. It was a short drive to the City View Condos, where he took up two parking spots because all the available spots were for compact vehicles.

The high-rise condo facility was two towers situated under a dimly-lit lobby and lounge area barely bright enough for Toney to navigate to the main elevators. He knew where she was in the Paradise Tower—the penthouse suite. The doors opened to an empty hallway with no sign of Jarvis being where he was supposed to be outside Tatyana's door.

If she decided to leave, he was supposed to report in and keep in touch about their whereabouts. Carl hadn't called back to report this, which meant they hadn't left or they did and Jarvis, for whatever reason, wasn't responding.

He knocked on the door several times and tried the outside buzzer. Nothing. He waited several minutes, even putting his ear to the door to see if he could hear any movement. Nothing.

Was Jarvis also messing around with the client? If he was, it was all Tatyana's doing. From his experience with her, she was not only a knockout, but she wasn't as passive as she came off as. He could tell she answered to the beat of her own drum. He could see her wanting some young boy toy to play with, no strings attached. Good for Jarvis if that was the case, but he was going to pay for it from Carl.

He tried the door handle and to his surprise found it unlocked. The room was dead quiet. The thunderstorm that ran through the city earlier was gone, leaving in its wake a kind of unsettling stillness.

He probed around for the nearest light switch and immediately regretted flicking it on. His eyes honed in on two bodies. The first was Jarvis, flat on his back, swollen tongue hanging out like dead bovine. The woman looked even worse. Her mouth was a bubbling fountain of blood. She couldn't have been dead for long.

His head buzzed as he thought about his next move. Call the cops? He didn't want to get caught up in answering a bunch of questions and being looked at as a possible suspect but he didn't have much of a choice. With a deep sigh, he took out his phone and called it in.

Chapter 36

It took only finding out where she worked for Detective Chase to figure out why he was being called out of bed to a double homicide at the City View Condos.

Tatyana Sokolov of the Lucky Hearts Casino was now the casino's third dead operations manager in less than a year. Even more interesting to Chase was who first called it in. Another run-in with Roddick's former partner and pal, Toney Bruzzone.

From early on, all signs looked like Tatyana's death was self-inflicted. As for the dead man not far from her. He had been strangled to death. He was a big guy, around six foot three, two hundred and twenty pounds. His muscular build showed he lifted heavy weights on a regular basis. Wrapped around his neck was a garrote wire made from guitar string tied around two wooden spools.

Toney was still at the scene being questioned by one of the night rotation detectives when Chase arrived and said the man's name was Jarvis and worked for the same executive protection agency as him.

"Murder-suicide?" McCarthy asked.

Chase turned to McCarthy who still looked half asleep.

"You think she got out of bed completely naked, went over, strangled her own bodyguard, who looks like he could deadlift a semi-truck and then shot herself?"

"Relax, I'm fucking with you. You see this?" McCarthy said, holding up a half-empty Styrofoam cup. "It's my second cup of coffee, and I'm still not awake. The next time you decide to get me out of bed, the least you could do is find me some Adderall."

Before Chase could reply, one of the officers came up to them.

"You two should come take a look at the security footage."

They took the elevator down to the ground floor and followed the officer down the hall to the security office.

The night security officer, who introduced himself as Jet, sat in front of a TV monitor while his supervisor, a broad-shouldered, portly, middle-aged man named Eugene Hylton, loomed right behind him. They had rewound the feed to where the time code was nearly two hours earlier.

The first feed they showed was from just inside the main entrance as a few tenants came in and out.

"What are we looking at here?" Chase asked.

"Just wait for it," Hylton said.

A few seconds later a figure stood inside the door frame, out of sight of the camera and seemed to be putting something on. They soon saw what it was when the figure stepped into camera view.

"Is that a rubber Elvis mask?" McCarthy asked.

"Looks like it," Eugene said in a straight, monotone voice.

Jet flipped the feed over to the corresponding camera inside the elevator, where the masked man stepped in and stood stoically as the car went up. The doors opened, and he stepped out. Rick sped the feed up a full forty minutes until the man stalked back into the elevator and they tracked him all the way to the lobby and out.

"And the King has left the building," McCarthy said.

Annoyed, Chase left the security office and started toward the main lobby when McCarthy caught up to him.

"I don't even have to ask, you think it's him."

"Of course, it's him."

"So he came here, strangled the hot, dead Russian lady's bodyguard and then made her kill herself?"

"She probably knew what was coming and figured offing herself was the better option."

McCarthy whistled. "You're building this guy up too much. He ain't the Devil."

"Close enough."

****

The petrichor from the wet creosote bushes after the previous night's thunderstorm gave the air a sweet, morning smell. It was cool enough to make Roddick and Kaylee have breakfast out on the patio before the temperature started to climb again.

"Did you see the news?" Kaylee asked between bites of her poached eggs.

"You mean the dead Russian from the Lucky Hearts Casino? Yeah, I read it. I warned her just the other day."

"They say it's a simple case of suicide."

"Suicide my ass," Roddick said, ripping into a chunk of bacon. "I know when police are not giving the full story to the press. Besides, I saw her. She wasn't suicidal. Far from it."

"You think it was the Scorpion?"

"Why else would they hold information back? Not only is he making the cops look bad but they don't want to admit to the press they can't collar a very dangerous man who's killed enough people in this town to fill a cemetery."

"Why kill her, though?"

"He's getting tired of waiting on us to get information. I knew he'd move in on her to get what he wanted."

"You think he got what he was looking for?"

"We'll know soon enough."

Kaylee cracked opened her first of what was sure to be many energy drinks of the day.

"Christ, you might as well just IV that shit into your veins."

"Like you have room to talk," she said, pointing to his third cup of coffee.

"Touché."

"You seem better," she said. "You're not getting as tired as fast."

"I feel better. Except I seem to forget stuff more easily than before. I completely forgot I'm hosting poker night tonight."

"Good to know. I'll see if Jessica is up for bowling or something."

"You could probably stick around if you want. You're pretty much one of the boys anyways."

Kaylee frowned. "I don't know if I should be insulted or not."

"If I were going for insulting you, I'd tell you how

much you remind me of your mother."

"Oh, fuck off."

Chapter 37

Kaylee got back early from bowling to find the boys gathered around the poker table underneath a plume of cigar smoke that smelled like chocolate.

"You're early," Roddick said.

"Jessica isn't much of a bowler. She spent most of her sets putting the ball in the gutter and flirting with the boys in the lane next to us."

"You can take my spot," Roddick said.

Kaylee grabbed a power drink from the fridge and took him up on the offer.

"What you boys playing? Texas Hold 'Em?"

"Yessir," Dennis said.

Dennis was a fellow PI friend of Roddick's. They would work cases together from time to time. Usually ones that involved around-the-clock surveillance. He was overweight and sweated a lot even when the AC was on. But he was nice, and Kaylee always got along with him.

Along with Shaun, the other person playing was Jacob, who worked with Shaun and Toney at the same high-end executive protection work. She was happy Toney wasn't there. He took his poker very seriously. He would follow T1000 blinds to the letter and raise the blind every 20 minutes on the dot. She'd never been able to sub if he was playing.

She looked at her dad's remaining chips and

couldn't help but feel a sense of loss that came with knowing some things would never be the same again. Before he had been shot, her dad was a very skilled poker player to where he once confessed to her, "I get great pleasure at taking money from smug assholes."

So good was he, he'd been kicked out of several casinos and disinvited to private poker events, to where he was content to just playing cards with friends. Now, he couldn't even do that.

Under-the-gun, Kaylee looked at her Ace-Queen and limped in by matching the big blind.

"So, you've been helping out your dad with the PI business he tells me," Shaun said.

"That's right."

"If you ever get tired of working for your dad, you can come work for me," Dennis said, with a wink before folding.

"There you go, already trying to steal my only employee," Roddick said.

Kaylee smiled. "It's okay, I don't think I could work for someone that doesn't believe in taking showers."

The crack got an all-around laugh as Jacob threw three community cards down: Qc, 9h, jd. Shaun bet ten chips and Kaylee called while Jacob folded. It was now just between Kaylee and Shaun at the Turn, as he put another community card down: ace of hearts. Kaylee bet five and Shaun stared hard at his hand.

"Aw, hell," he grumbled, tossing his cards down.

"She got you." Jacob laughed.

"I think you brought in a ringer," Dennis said.

"I think so," Shaun said as he stood up. "I need another beer."

"You stay there, I'll get it," Roddick said.

Roddick had started toward the kitchen when the doorbell rang.

"Did one of you order a pizza?" Dennis asked.

Roddick went to the door, hoping it wasn't an angry neighbor. They weren't being that loud. It was Detective Chase. He was in his motorcycle jacket, which seemed strange to Roddick since it was so warm out. He looked up over Chase's shoulder and saw his Ducati parked at the end of the drive.

"Hey, Joe."

"Detective Chase, what brings you by? Out for a spin?"

"It's Jeff, I'm off duty, and yeah, just needed to go for a ride."

"Come in. We're just winding up poker night."

"No, it's okay. I don't to want to intrude. I'll only be a minute. I was in the area and thought I'd ask you about Tatyana Sokolov, the Russian woman that worked for the Lucky Hearts Casino. I'm sure you already read about it."

"Yeah," Roddick replied. "Shaun filled me in some more since she was one of their clients and Toney found her."

Chase nodded. "Did you ever speak to her?"

"Yes. Twice."

"What did you talk about?"

"The first time was shortly after I started working again. Thought I'd go and see who was running the place."

"And the second time."

Roddick was more hesitant. He didn't want to tell him that he went to warn her about the possibility of the

185

Scorpion coming after her. He didn't need to implicate himself in this psycho's criminal activities.

"Just a business check-in. Seeing if the casino needed any work from me. Like what I did for them in the past."

Chase jerked a nod. Roddick wasn't sure if he bought his explanation or not.

"Well, I'll let you get back to your poker night."

"You're more than welcome to join in."

"No, I got to get into work early tomorrow."

Chase started putting his helmet on as he walked down the drive toward his bike. When he heard the door shut, he slipped it off and set the helmet on the seat before brandishing a plastic evidence bag from inside his coat.

He strode discreetly over to the side of the house and flipped open the blue recycle bin. He rummaged around in it before seeing what he was after and with the plastic bag, pulled out an empty power drink can. He sealed it up in the bag and stuffed it in his inside pocket.

He could hear music playing in the house as he pressed the electronic ignition and throttled out of the driveway.

****

He sat in his den with only a 24-inch neon wall sign of poker cards and chips for light. On the shelves and walls were framed pictures of him in the military mixed with him standing next to celebrities and athletes, many of them A-listers.

Carl prided himself in his work. There wasn't a training program in the area he either didn't take part in or teach. Like the military, it was all business to him, and he made it clear to keep it as such. It was all too easy for bodyguards protecting VIPs to become part of their entourage, to where you stop doing your job and become nothing but a glorified luggage handler or dog walker.

Most of his clients respected his professionalism and the results. Though at first, many of them balked at his demands. Such as him approving all social media posts when they were on the move to make sure they weren't giving clues to where they were, or the post didn't geotag their exact location. Because of these precautions, he had few run-ins with stalkers and fanatics.

But now, one of his men was dead along with one of his clients. Though he had only known her briefly, he had liked Tatyana.

The fifth of Jack he was drinking wasn't helping his mood. Not even the two escorts who were sleeping in his bed had helped. He hated failure. And this was a big one. He didn't get his business from advertisement but by word of mouth. This wasn't going to be good word of mouth.

When his clients at the Lucky Hearts Casino had let him in on the information that they had hired a professional to take care of some loose ends, he was against it. He knew they wouldn't hire a run of the mill novice or journeyman but a legit pro and that's exactly who they got.

Though Tatyana never gave him the whole story on what they did to piss this guy off, he figured it probably had to do with money. You had to be pretty stupid or ballsy to rip off a professional killer of this caliber. Now, this psycho was running roughshod over the entire casino and his reputation. There was no way he was going to sit by and let that happen.

The only option he had to salvage himself would be to take this killer out himself. But first, he had to find him. He had plenty of connections, so that shouldn't be too hard. This hired killer might be a professional at taking out scrubs and defenseless women, but he was sure he hadn't gone up against someone with Carl's type of training and skill. This hotshot was going to be in for a real surprise.

Chapter 38

Detective Chase and McCartney got to the precinct early and hadn't even reached their desks when their sergeant told them Lieutenant Cervantes wanted to see both of them.

"Well, this is going to be interesting," McCarthy said as they walked toward the lieutenant's office.

Lieutenant Christopher Cervantes was sitting behind a desk full of papers and blotter. He was dressed in a blue dress shirt, plaid necktie, and dress pants. He had a full, plump face and a dark goatee, and thin, graying hair. Behind him was a wooden bookshelf that held police code policy binders and clipboards. The surrounding walls had various sizes of postcards, one of them in the shape of a heart that read *World's Best Dad*. Next to it were several magnetic bulldog clips that held memorandums he had highlighted.

"You wanted to see us, Sir," Chase said.

"Yes. I'll get straight to the point. Do you think your hitman is back?"

He was looking right at Chase.

"It appears so, Sir."

"And do you think he's responsible for the homicides at the City View Condos?"

"Yes."

Lt. Cervantes cleared his throat to draw attention to what he was about to say next.

"Very well. What do you need as far as resources in order to apprehend your suspect?"

Chase and McCarthy looked confused. This was not what they were expecting to hear.

"Is something wrong, detectives?"

"No, Sir. Why the sudden urgency?"

Lt. Cervantes shuffled through his stack of papers until he found the one he was looking for and handed it to Chase. It was a print out from yesterday's front page of the *Las Vegas Review*.

Clark County's Unsolved Murder Rate of 57% Falls Below National Average of 63%.

Seemed even the local media couldn't whitewash what looked like incompetence from the Metro PD.

"Kind of hard to close cases when your hands are constantly being tied," Chase said.

"That's not an excuse. Every officer that makes the decision to work in this town knows there's politics at play."

Chase caught a glance from McCarthy that told him to let it go.

"With all due respect, Sir. We could have possibly apprehended our suspect months ago, but the department seemed more willing to sweep his string of murders under the rug as nothing but gang violence. We still haven't been able to get a warrant to fully question and search the Lucky Hearts Casino, who by all accounts contracted this killer."

"Close the door," Lt. Cervantes said to McCarthy as he stood up and came around to the front of the desk.

"Let me make it clear to you two gentlemen. This is coming all the way from the fucking top. They want this hitman, or whoever the hell he is, apprehended and fast before it draws full national media attention."

"Oh, we wouldn't want that," Chase said.

"What was that, Detective?"

Lt. Cervantes stood close enough to Chase's face he could smell the halitosis on Cervantes' breath.

Trying not to gag, Chase said, "I didn't say anything."

"Good. Now get the fuck out. Both of you."

****

The Scorpion parked the Impala off Allen facing toward Cheyenne Avenue. He'd been there for a while when his GPS monitor dinged, signaling his target was moving. He started the Impala and had it up to sixty in less than six seconds as he shot onto Cheyenne with enough torque from the engine that it nearly lifted the front end off the road.

The Impala caught up to the Nissan Maxima as it turned left onto north MLK Boulevard. The Scorpion kept his distance as he listened to the engine hum. They stayed on MLK for over four miles before the Maxima took a left on I-15 and stayed on it until getting off at exit 37.

The exit fed out onto Tropicana where his prey made a left onto Dean Martin Drive and pulled into a mid level family hotel.

The Scorpion parked and watched as the cop got out and walked up the outside L-shaped stairs to the second floor.

The Scorpion followed all the way up to the second landing to see a door down the outside hallway shut. Room 238. He stood in front of the door and examined the hinges to see which way it opened. It swung inward.

There were muffled sounds of arguing going on

inside, but the Scorpion didn't bother to try to make it out. He went back to his machine and waited. The temperature was well over one hundred. Too hot not to have the AC on. He checked the gas level. He'd already drained through a quarter tank running the AC. Small price to pay to keep from burning alive in your own car.

Twenty or so minutes went by before the cop came back down. He had a look of irritation as he climbed back into the Nissan Maxima and sped off.

The Scorpion opened the glove compartment and grabbed a pair of gloves and a Glock. He switched out its barrel with a threaded one and screwed on a suppressor. He reached the stairs as one of the ground floor room doors opened and an underage-looking Mexican girl came out with a much older man wearing nothing but shorts and flip-flops.

The Scorpion kept out of view on the landing and waited as he slipped her some money and she stuffed it in the back pocket of her jean shorts that barely covered her ass.

Nobody was on the second-floor walkway. He could hear a woman crying from one of the rooms as he passed by. The sound of a TV from another. There was no noise coming from 238. He tried the door to make sure it was locked. It was. He pulled the Glock out and kicked the door near the locking mechanism. Chunks of splintered wood broke off as the door swung open.

The two men inside had no time to react as the Scorpion fired. The suppressed Glock sounded like a nail gun as he put two slugs in the nearest man's skull. The pinging sound of ejected casing hit the floor as the other man, who was sitting on the couch, reached for a Ruger 9mm. The Scorpion fired, and the man's head smacked against the retaining wall and slumped over.

The Scorpion caught movement out of the corner of his left eye when he had first breached the door, and without hesitating, he emptied the magazine into the sliding bathroom door. There was a loud thud followed by pinging. He reloaded and waited.

People were yelling outside. Even with a suppressor, repeated gunshots were loud enough to draw attention. With his left hand, he slid the bathroom door open. An East European man was sprawled out, dead, inside a small fiberglass tub/shower. He had tried to grab the shower curtain but tore half of it off the hooks.

On the raised wash basin was an assortment of drug paraphernalia. A small glass vial, pipe, tin foil, a couple of crusty spoons, mirror, straw, razor blade, a lighter, and pill bottles. The other two dead men were also of the East European/Russian type. The one on the couch was watching cartoons.

There were two twin beds and on one of them was a stockpile of weapons and ammo. AK-47s, a Barrett .50 caliber, shotguns, handguns of all variety and caliber, zip gun, and high capacity magazines and ammo. Some of the magazines were even clamped together jungle style.

The room was a candy store for anyone in need of illegal weapons but who was the Candyman? That's who the Scorpion wanted to know. He walked around the bed and saw several duffel bags. He didn't need to open them to know what was inside. On the small round table next to the wall were a couple empty beer bottles, a coffee maker, and a small microwave. He could smell that something had just been heated in it and opened the door. Inside was a still warm hot-pocket.

The commotion outside was picking up. It was time for him to go. He unscrewed the suppressor from the Glock and tossed the gun into the pile of weapons on the bed. He took the pizza pocket, one of the duffel bags and walked out, leaving the door open.

A woman screaming along with a man shouting could be heard as he closed in on the Impala . He threw the duffel in the back seat, bit into the hot-pocket, and pulled out casually.

****

Kaylee stepped into the three-story tube slide at the Golden Nugget Casino, got into the supine position, and let go. She picked up speed as the tube became blue and it went straight through the casino's 200,000-gallon shark tank.

She spilled out into a pool where Jessica was lying across one of the lounge chairs in the water. She had blown up Kaylee's phone to go to the pool. Kaylee relented because the heat was getting to be too much even with the AC blasting.

"I hit my head going down," Jessica said.

She had gone head first as if she was trying out for the Olympic Skeleton team.

"That's what you get," Kaylee said.

A couple of local Freemont street drunks were at the poolside bar already filling up on their afternoon nerve toxins and whistling at the women as they stepped out of the pool to towel off.

"Pigs," Jessica said.

"When you wear next to nothing to go swimming it's kind of hard not to expect that kind of reaction."

Jessica rolled her eyes. The drunks kept catcalling until a casino employee told them to leave. That only left a few patrons at the bar. One of them was watching them. It became more outright as the bar crowd thinned out even more.

"That older, dark-haired guy is staring at you," Jessica whispered through the side of her mouth.

Kaylee turned to look.

"I think he was following me here."

"You should call security and get him thrown out. He's probably one of those sex traffickers."

"Let me go ask," Kaylee said as she stood up and started walking toward him. Jessica yelled at her to come back, but Kaylee ignored her. The dark-haired man was good looking for his age. He was the strong, pretty-boy type she saw all the time at the gym. Except he looked like he kept in shape for more than just appearances.

He didn't seem at all caught off guard that she was coming straight toward him, almost like he was expecting her to.

"Can I help you?" she asked.

Carl took off his mirrored sunglasses and smiled.

"That depends."

"On what?"

"On whether or not you can let me talk to your friend."

"My friend?"

The bartender handed him a rum punch. He tossed the fruity umbrella it came with to the side and downed the drink before signaling for another.

"You know who I'm talking about. See, I have a lot of connections in this city. Even with some bad

Armenian folks. They told me some colleagues of theirs used this red-haired girl as bait to lure in this psycho hitman. Didn't take a whole lot of inquiring to figure out the girl was you."

"That plan didn't work out so well for them. You think you can do better?"

Carl smiled, showing off a perfect set of white teeth. *Veneers for sure.*

"I'm going for a more diplomatic approach."

"Why do you want to talk to him so bad anyways?"

"He killed an employee of mine and one of my clients. A woman, if that means anything to you."

"Should it?" Kaylee crossed her arms over her chest, still acting nonchalant and not enjoying this one bit.

"Only if you think it'll protect you."

"I'm quite aware he doesn't discriminate."

"And you're okay with that?" He said it like it should matter.

"Did I say I was? Last time I saw him, I put two bullets into him. That should tell you right there he ain't my friend."

He raised an eyebrow in surprise. "Did you now?"

"Yeah." She half-smiled, but still not too cocky to know she had gotten lucky.

"You know what I found interesting when I did my inquiring? There was no mention of you with the police. It's as if they weren't aware of your involvement in the massacre that took place at a villa earlier this year."

Kaylee scowled. The son of a bitch was good-looking and smart, a bad combination. She turned to see how Jessica was doing. Just fine, apparently. She was

196

talking to some young, tatted up stud, who had come down the slide.

She turned her attention back to Carl. "You just want to talk to him?"

"That's right."

"Is this dead woman client of yours worth getting yourself killed over?"

Carl finished his second drink and set it down with a laugh. "I ain't afraid. If anything, he should really be afraid of me."

It was Kaylee's turn to laugh. "You? I don't think so. Trust me when I tell you, this man is very good at killing people."

"You some kind of fan of his?"

"No. But I've seen first-hand what he can do."

"I'm going to let you in on a secret. He may be good, but I'm better."

Chapter 39

The amount of ATF agents inside and outside of the Holiday Inn made the place look like Waco.

The bodies had long been removed, and Chase was left watching as the agents collected and inventoried all the weapons.

There was blood everywhere. The couch and bathroom were covered in it. The excessive heat had turned the pools of the stuff into a gluey paste like spoiled marinara. The forensic boys had their work cut out for them.

One of the officers came up to Chase.

"Bagged all the drugs in the bathroom."

"Good. Take it down to the lab to get tested."

Chase followed the officer outside and walked over to one of the detectives interviewing a neighbor. A middle-aged man, late forties. Brown hair, and tortoiseshell glasses.

"I just checked in last night. I traveled here on business."

"What do you do for work, Mister Seiler?" the detective asked.

"I'm a sales rep for an industrial manufacturing company." He looked around, agitated, probably worried the hitman would come back and take care of him for talking to the cops.

"About what time did you check-in?"

"Around one a.m. I had a long meeting in LA and didn't leave until late."

"And you said you woke up hearing what sounded like gunshots?"

"That's right."

"What time?"

"A little past noon I'd say."

"Can you describe what the gun shots sounded like?"

"I can tell you they were using some kind of suppressor. I know my way around guns, and the shots were muffled."

Chase let the detective finish his questioning and went back inside. Agent Landry came up to him. He was decked out in a blue t-shirt and IIIA bulletproof vest that read ATF Police and a blue ATF ball cap, just in case anybody was unclear what branch he was from.

"So we collected about 25 handguns, 40 rifles, five shotguns, three AK-47s, a Barrett .50 caliber, over a 100 high capacity magazines, and a couple thousand rounds of ammo."

"Were any of the handguns a Glock?" Chase asked.

"I believe one or two were."

"Let me see."

They went to the bed where the handguns were piled up to be collected. Chase slapped on a pair of latex gloves and rooted through them until he found it. Built in the same kit fashion as the others, which meant like the others, no serial number. Remembering what the man said about a suppressor, he examined the barrel. Threaded.

"That's the murder weapon right there."

He signaled for an officer to bag it as Agent

Landry pulled him aside.

"What exactly are we dealing with here?" Landry asked.

"What do you mean, Agent?"

"I mean, who goes in, shoots three guys who look like Russian mafia and leaves this stockpile of weapons and a duffel with two million dollars beside the bed?"

"You tell me. What do you think these weapons are for?"

"Your guess is as good as mine, Detective. Could be selling them off to Mexicans. We've been picking up a lot of arms trafficking here because of the crackdown in Arizona and California."

"Are the Mexican cartels doing business with the Russians?"

"They'll do business with anyone that will get them weapons."

He was right. A couple of months back a fast food restaurant manager with a wife and two kids and no ties to Mexico whatsoever, was sentenced to eighteen years for buying guns for the Los Zetas cartel. He wanted the money, and they wanted the guns.

"You seem to have a pretty good idea who is behind this," Agent Landry said. "A hitman?"

Chase nodded. "I'd imagine you're familiar with them."

"Afraid so. Just a few months back we helped the Mexican police catch this hitman they called, "the Soup Maker," because he'd boil the remains of his victims in barrels of acid until there was nothing left of them but this soupy shit."

"Christ," Chase said. "We really are sheep amongst wolves."

****

When Kaylee was with the Scorpion at the motel during the periods he went off to gather weapons, he had given her an anonymous virtual number to text him. Now, she needed to get a hold of him, so she sent a text earlier in the evening asking for a callback. It was a long shot since he likely changed the number.

With no direct reply, she spent the rest of the evening in, eating pizza and playing pool with her dad. Though, it ended up being yet another reminder that Roddick was no longer what he once was. He couldn't think ahead enough to set up his next shot. After beating him badly in the first two games, she tried to go easier on him, which only irritated him.

"I know what you're doing," he said.

He noticed she had purposely set him up for an easy side pocket shot, which he ended up scratching. Frustrated at his limitations, he let his stick bounce off the ground before calling it a night.

Seeing a man who could once do almost anything, now handicapped, was enough to bring out a bitter rage against the person responsible for it. She was glad he hadn't called her back. She would have let him have it.

She listened to trance music in her room until she calmed herself down enough to go to sleep. No sooner did it seem like she hit the pillow her phone rang. She reached for it off the night stand: 3:32 a.m.-.unknown caller.

" 'Course you would call me this late," she said.

There was no reply.

"Right, not one for small talk. There's a guy looking for you."

"Who?"

"Hold on," she said, as she got up and grabbed her wallet. It took her a moment to fish out the business card Carl had given her.

"His name is Carl Maldonado. His number is 702-884-0081."

"What does he got to do with you?" the Scorpion asked.

"Nothing. He followed me. Says he does 'executive protection' work. I guess he was the bodyguard to some woman you killed. Now he wants to get a hold of you. And he pretty much tried to blackmail me to do it."

"So you want me to take care of him for you?"

"I didn't say that. I told him it was a bad idea. He didn't look like someone that takes no for an answer. I'm just fulfilling my part. Do with it as you will."

"There's something else."

"Yes, whatever happens, promise me you will keep my father out of it. You've already done enough harm. He isn't even half of what he used to be because of you."

"Why would I promise you anything?"

"Because I know more about you than you think."

"That so."

"Yes. How was the weather in Chicago when you murdered Arthur Cook?"

If her big reveal of information about him had caught the Scorpion off guard, he didn't show it.

"It was cold."

"Bet you don't even care that his wife killed herself over what you did."

"If she did, it was because she couldn't handle the reality of her actions."

"What do you mean?"

"Who do you think hired me?"

"Bullshit. His own daughter said he was into drugs and owed some dealers a lot of money."

"Unknown drug dealers always make good strawmen to pin murders on. Especially ones done by bitter wives who catch their husbands cheating on them with much younger models."

"Why are you telling me this?"

"It's what you wanted to know, isn't it? You said so yourself, she's dead. I owe no loyalty to a dead woman."

"You're a fuckin' monster."

The line went dead. In a fit of fury, Kaylee threw her phone across the room and screamed into her pillow so that her dad couldn't hear her.

****

Kaylee's sleepless night left her half-awake as she steered her car to her dad's office.

Roddick had an early meeting with some insurance company execs about getting workers' comp cases. This left her alone for the morning to do background checks and accumulate the 10,000 experience hours required by the Nevada Licensing Board if she decided to get her investigator license when she turned twenty-one.

She wasn't expecting to see Detective Chase waiting for her as she pulled in. He was standing by the door and walked up to her as soon as she stepped out of her car.

"Sorry, my dad won't be in until this afternoon."

"Actually, I'm here to talk to you."

Seemed like lately everybody wanted to talk to her.

"Do you mind if I grab something to eat first? I didn't have breakfast."

"Of course. I was actually about to grab a coffee myself."

He followed her into the donut shop, where she ordered a bacon, egg, cheese croissant and a hash brown while he went for a plain medium coffee and a couple donuts.

The place was pretty quiet except for the occasional construction worker coming in for a quick order. Chase found an empty booth and gestured for them to sit down.

His coffee was too hot to drink right away, so he removed the lid and a burst of steam came out like a blown radiator hose.

"They say drinking warm drinks when it's hot out actually cools you down," Chase said.

"Yeah, well, whoever said that never lived in Nevada."

Kaylee pulled out a power drink from her backpack and cracked it open. Chase tried to hide his smile as he looked at the can.

Between bites of her croissant, she asked, "What did you want to talk to me about?"

Chase dunked his donut into his coffee and took a bite and thought about how to best approach what he was about to say.

"I obtained your fingerprints and ran them against some of the ones we found at a couple crime scenes. They matched a partial we recovered at the Satellite Motel where we found two dead Armenian gang members."

Kaylee put her breakfast sandwich down and

scowled. "What do you mean you obtained my fingerprints? I don't recall ever submitting my fingerprints to anything."

Chase leaned straight back in the booth and rubbed his hand across his face. "I, er, might have gotten them from your trash. More specifically, off a can of one them energy drinks you like so much."

"So, you illegally obtained them?"

"Look, that's not the point. I'm not here to bust you. I just want to know the truth. Were you at that motel and did you go off with who I think is a very dangerous killer?"

She wanted to tell him the truth, but that would be admitting to intentionally being an accessory to murder.

"Some girls and I from the university go to that motel from time to time to party. They don't seem to clean the place very well, so no doubt my prints got left behind."

Chase took a cautious sip of his coffee.

"You don't seem like the party girl type."

"When in Rome," she said.

"Is that the story you're going to stick with?"

"Afraid so."

"I don't know how involved you are, but it would be in your best interests if you were honest with me. Because if I find more linking you with my suspect, it won't be a friendly social call next time."

"I'm aware of that, Detective."

He nodded and was about to get up to leave when he asked, "What's he like?"

Kaylee's eyes flickered. "Excuse me?"

"You heard me. What's he like?"

"I'm afraid I don't know who you're talking

about."

"Sure you don't," he said and left.

Kaylee sat for a good amount of time alone in the booth. She wasn't even licensed yet and already she was on the bad side of law enforcement. Her mind raced on how Chase found her out.

It wouldn't have been Carl, because that was the leverage he was holding over her. It had to be someone at the Satellite or Sandman Motel. But how? She was wearing a wig. Maybe she should've been extra cautious and concealed her freckles. Or maybe she just needed a better wig.

Regardless, he was on to her now. Her best chance of steering him away from her was by putting him on the path toward the Scorpion. And that's what she was going to do.

Chapter 40

The weights hit the rubber floor and sank in. Carl had just finished his last set of dumbbell chest butterflies to the point of muscle overload. He tried to make a fist, but it only brought on a fit of spasms.

He sat up from the bench and wiped his sweaty palms on his dingy shorts. Though he was listening to his own workout music, he could still hear the grunts of other large men throwing weights around until they were physically spent.

It was Carl's kind of gym. Dirty, loud, with rusted weights and buckets of baby powder. The kind of place where men went to work out and the exact opposite of the clean and feminine gyms the bigger franchises ran.

He racked the dumbbells and was reaching for another set when his phone buzzed inside his pocket. Unknown caller. He smiled.

"You wanted to talk to me."

"I'm disappointed," Carl said. "You're not even using one of those voice disguisers."

"There's no point in that."

"Oh, why not?"

"Because one of us isn't going to be alive for much longer."

"Now, wait a minute. No need to go to that extreme. I just wanted to talk to the man that killed one of my best men and a very lovely client of mine."

"That's not all you want."

Carl looked around. The usual crowd was working out. One of the big guys he knew was walking by him doing a farmer's haul carrying 140 pounds in each hand. The other remaining members he knew and even spotted for and vice versa. Nothing unusual. Yet he couldn't shake the feeling he had eyes on him.

"I'll admit, I did want put the hurt on you for all the trouble you've caused me. But now that I've had time to cool my head, I just want to talk."

"Just want to talk," the Scorpion repeated.

"That's right."

"Tell me, do I sound like a fool to you?"

"Look, it ain't like that. No tricks. From one professional to another."

The sound of weights hitting the floor shook Carl as he waited for the Scorpion to respond. Carl turned to see a humongous bearded brute that looked like a Nordic Viking pounding his chest in celebration for what he had managed to lift.

"You still there?" Carl asked.

"Where do you want to meet?"

****

Carl walked into the restaurant and found a booth that faced the front entrance. He looked around and saw only older people eating their mid-afternoon dinner. It was an odd-style place with walls covered in antiques and vintage photographs and polished brass accent furniture, Tiffany-style lamp fixtures for lighting, and checkered floor and table clothes.

The waitresses all knew Carl. He was a regular and usually came in for a slice of pie. Today was no exception.

A young, curly-haired brunette in a red shirt with one pocket, black slacks, and non-slip shoes came by. Her name tag read *Keri* but he already knew that.

"Hey, you," she said. "Just getting pie today?"

"No, I'm expecting someone, so better bring a menu. And yes, I will take a slice of your key lime."

"Coming right up."

Carl watched as she walked off. *Cute.* Some other time, perhaps. He looked out at the parking lot and watched as a UPS truck pulled up. He checked his phone. 4:55 p.m. He'd told him five exactly and didn't expect someone like the Scorpion to be late.

Keri came back and set down two menus, the key lime, and two glasses of water. He sipped the water and stuck a fork in the pie. The best. Things were already turning around and soon they would even more.

He'd been planning it out for days. The Scorpion would show up, they'd have a nice little talk, and then he'd wait for him to leave. Outside he had two of his guys, boys he'd served with, waiting for him. As soon as the Scorpion reached his car they were told to take him out.

Snap a couple pictures of their handiwork so he could show off to his former clients, and he'd be back in business. Easy-peasy.

He had finished his pie when someone put a Johnny Cash song on the jukebox. He listened to it for a moment and lost track of time.

He checked his phone again. 5:03 p.m. He was late. Carl looked around again. Same old people and a young family were eating. Keri came back.

"Would you like something to drink besides water while you wait?"

"Best not, darlin'," he said.

"Oh, it's one of those types of meet-ups," she said.

"Afraid so. Business. But after it's wrapped up, I'd like to take you out sometime."

She blushed and smiled. "I'd like that."

She went to attend to another order as Carl glanced out the front window again. Nothing but a heavy late afternoon commute on the main road.

He started dialing one of his men outside when a homeless man that looked like Charlie Manson walked in. He had the widely-opened eyelids of a crazed man with a brown bird's nest of a beard and barely dressed in a ripped, stained t-shirt, and jeans.

The man looked around the place in a confused manner until he saw Carl. He staggered up to Carl's table and stood there for a moment.

"Something I can do for you?" Carl asked.

The crazed man's speech was disorganized as he mostly mumbled to himself while looking at nothing in particular. Carl sighed with impatience.

"Listen, buddy, I'm about to meet someone, so can you either get on with it or get out. I'll see if I can get you a few bucks when I leave."

The man kept mumbling. Carl started to stand up when the man reached into his pocket and dropped two wallets on the table.

Carl stared at them for a moment. One of them was an olive green tri-fold wallet with a small American flag sewed onto it while the other looked like a mini military bag. Both looked familiar. Carl kept his hands from shaking as he opened up the tri-fold wallet and pulled out the Nevada driver's license: Derrick Burch— Veteran.

"Who gave you this?" Carl yelled as he sprung to his feet and grabbed the homeless man. The man kept mumbling.

"Who, Goddamn it!"

Keri came rushing up as everyone turned to look to see what was going on.

"Let go of him" she pleaded.

Carl ignored her and started to lift the man up off his feet.

"Tell me!"

"He…paid me to gib you dis—"

"Who paid you?"

"I dunno!"

Carl let go of him, and the bum fell to the floor for a moment before getting back on his feet and running out. A ringing filled Carl's ears and his heart felt like a scared rat clawing its way out of his chest.

He had killed both of them while he sat there eating pie.

Sweat dampened his face as the feeling of wanting to throw up came over him.

"Are you okay?" Keri asked.

He cursed to himself. Obviously, he wasn't okay. He looked outside and saw nothing. Yet he knew the bastard was out there waiting for him.

"I'm calling the police," another waitress yelled.

Carl turned and started heading toward the kitchen.

"You can't come back here," a young chef said as he tried to block him. Carl ran straight through him like it was an Oklahoma drill, sending the guy straight into the wall.

Carl saw the back door and ran to it. Outside, two Asians were starting to offload produce from a refrigerated truck onto hand carts. Almost knocking one of the carts over, one of the Asians started cursing Carl as he fled.

The adjoining lot was a home improvement store with construction trucks pulling in and out full of lumber and housing materials. Carl ran behind the building and kept going through a few commercial lots until he connected to a back neighborhood.

He stood on the sidewalk underneath shade from some palms and tried to catch his breath. His whole body was bathed in sweat. He kept walking until he saw some old woman watering plants. He grabbed the hose from her and drank from it. The woman said nothing. *Senile.* When he finished, he dropped the hose and kept going.

An orange Fat Daddy's ice cream truck with a giant ice cream cone on top of it crept past him while ominously playing, "Turkey in the Straw." The surrealness of it all was almost too much for Carl but he kept walking. He'd find the nearest bus stop and bus his way home. Tomorrow he'd come back and get his car.

His stomach finally settled down as he no longer felt the need to throw up. He took several deep breaths of the dry heat and tried to get his heart to slow down. Even though it was hot as hell out, the walking seemed to help. A few blocks down he could see the sign for the 102 bus.

He smiled as he started to cross a passing street. A figure stepped out in front of him. All he could make out was the short, spiky blondish hair, and sunglasses. Carl reached for his FNX .45 from his paddle holster.

A shiny, metallic object reflected the sun into his eyes as the feeling of being slapped shook him. He looked down and saw blood draining out from his armpit and stomach. The flashing kept going as a sense of coldness came over Carl. His vision blurred as the sidewalk came crashing in on him.

Chapter 41

The morning crowd at the Spin-City laundromat was thinning out as Roddick sat in one of the waiting chairs. He was watching a tattooed, white-trash woman in a jean skirt and tank top with an eagle on it. She claimed her back hurt so badly from an injury at work that she couldn't even get out of bed. Yet here she was carrying two large garbage bags full of clothes to one of the commercial washers.

He was recording her on his phone the same way he had recorded her the previous day going to a country bar, where she spent her time playing darts and dancing to some Patsy Cline songs before going home with some fat cowboy in a ten-gallon hat.

Roddick had seen it all doing workers' comp cases. A guy claiming neck injury teaching a rock climbing course on the weekends or a man with a supposed broken back building a deck in his yard.

Before his own injury, Roddick had hated taking these types of cases. It often meant spending hours and even days on surveillance doing nothing. But now he enjoyed it. It didn't require him to sit at a computer going through documents or reports, which mentally exhausted him now.

His doctor kept telling him his mental stamina might improve, but he was starting to doubt it. He needed to accept he was never going to be the same person he was before getting shot, and try to work around it.

The woman finished loading the washer and was now feeding it quarters. When it started, she took a seat a few spots down from him and looked up at one of the TVs. The morning news was on.

Roddick glanced up and watched the top stories of the day. One of them was a multiple-stabbing fatality. Roddick didn't pay it much attention until they showed a picture of the vic. It was Carl Maldonado. Toney and Shaun's boss.

Roddick had first met him during a poker night that Toney was hosting. He didn't think much of him. He just remembered Carl spending most of the night talking about all the hot women he had "smashed" that week.

He was so transfixed on the TV trying to hear what the reporter was saying about the murder he hadn't realized the woman left. He glanced around the laundromat but she wasn't there. No matter. She'd have to come back to switch her clothes to the dryer.

Slightly annoyed that he let her slip out, he looked up at the TV again. They had moved on to the weather report. More hot weather. What a shocker. His phone rang. Mickey Blundell.

"Hello, Mickey," he said.

"Hey, Joe. You busy right now?"

"That depends. What's up?"

"Meet me at Stefano's in an hour."

The called ended before Roddick even had time to respond back. So much for waiting for her to come back. Not that it mattered, he had more than enough video evidence to send to the insurance agent handling her case.

He got to the door and that old feeling he used to get when he was a patrol cop, and could tell he was being watched, came over him. He turned and darted his eyes around the place. The only people waiting for their clothes were a young, homeless-looking couple, a fat Hispanic woman with three kids, and one of the attendants pushing a large laundry cart. He shrugged the feeling off. *Carl getting knifed must have put me on edge.*

Moments after Roddick left the laundromat, the bathroom door opened and the Scorpion, dressed in a ball cap and sunglasses, stepped out. He went up to the washing machine the woman had filled and stared at his shimmering reflection as the clothes spun.

"There a reason you're staring at my clothes? I've already had enough pervs stealin' my panties."

The Scorpion shifted around and glared at the woman Roddick had been following. It was enough for her to take a step back while giving a nervous smile that showed a mouthful of missing teeth.

"I was just kiddin'," she said.

The woman had been around bad men all her life. Men that beat her, raped her, put out cigarettes on her when they were bored. None of them scared her though. Except for this man. He had the look of the devil. She kept moving backward until she bumped into another woman folding clothes on a countertop.

"Hey, watch where you're goin'!"

"Sorry," she mumbled, as she pivoted and headed straight out the side door.

The Scorpion hadn't moved. He had simply observed the woman's behavior with contempt.

****

Stefano's was a wood fire pizzeria and pub off Del Rey. Roddick followed a waitress, holding a pizza peel that looked like a snow shovel to Mickey's table. She set his order down.

It was a Brooklyn-style pie with a thin, slightly burnt crispy crust from the added cornmeal. Roddick sat down and ordered a beer from the waitress before grabbing a slice of the pizza.

"This place makes better pizza than New York," Mickey said.

"Well, Stefano is from New York, so…"

"That's my point. New York can't even keep their own talent. Why? Because it's an over-populated, over-expensive dump. The last time I was there I thought I was in a third world country."

"You ain't goin' to hear any objections from me."

" 'Course not. I'm talking to a New Englander."

The waitress came back with Roddick's beer. The glass was already sweating as he gulped a good portion of it down.

"What did you want to see me about?"

"You wanted to know the goings-on at the Lucky Hearts Casino, right?"

"That's right."

"I was there this morning and was talking to someone I know who works there. Not going to name names, of course. But he told me management is all shook up, and the big shots are coming in for some meeting tonight."

"Where?"

"Private cabin at Mount Charleston. I got a good idea which one because I think I went there once for a private poker game. A real nice place, if it's the one I'm thinking of."

"Probably is. Does your friend have any idea what's got them all stirred up?"

Mickey shook his head.

"No. But I'd imagine it has to do with all these killings going on in their ranks. Word is, our friend the Scorpion is behind it."

"It appears so."

Mickey dusted the pizza crumbs off his hands and smirked.

"You already know this?"

"Yes."

"You've spoken to him, haven't you?"

Roddick finished his beer and said, "More or less. I wouldn't say it was much of a conversation."

"What did he want with you?"

"Information."

"On the Lucky Hearts Casino? Is that why you came to see me? You helping him out?"

"It's a little more complicated than me just helping him out. We're talking about the son of a bitch that shot me."

"He threatened to finish the job if you didn't help him?"

"You're too smart for me, Mickey."

Roddick was starting to get uncomfortable at Mickey's line of questioning.

"You think you can get me directions to where this cabin is?"

"You really going to go out there?"

"Yes."

"You sure that's a good idea? I mean, after your

injury and all?"

"I'll be fine."

"If you say so." Mickey didn't sound convinced but drew out a rudimentary map on one of the napkins.

"Thanks, Mickey," Roddick said, dropping a twenty that more than covered his portion of the bill.

****

Kaylee knew her dad was up to something when he arrived with Chinese take-out for dinner.

"I'm going out tonight," he said, setting the food on the kitchen countertop.

"Is it for that workers' comp case you're doing or a night out with the boys?" she asked.

"Work."

He took out two plates and filled them with chow mein with shrimp, kung pao chicken, and Mongolian beef. Kaylee grabbed a beer out the fridge and a power drink, and they sat at the table. It was too hot outside to eat out on the patio.

They ate mostly in silence until Roddick left to use the bathroom. Kaylee pounced on his phone that he'd left beside his plate. She knew all the passwords he used and got into it fast.

She first went to his call log. Mickey's number popped right out. She checked his messages, but they were cleared along with his search history. She tried his map app and saw he had recently put in an address near Kyle Canyon Road. Hearing footsteps, she exited out and set the phone back where it was as Roddick walked back into the kitchen and sat back down.

"So, I've been thinking a lot," Kaylee said between bites. "Of not going back to school this fall and just continue helping you out with work."

The comment caused him to set his fork down. "Did you tell your mother this?"

"No, not yet."

"Good. I don't need to hear her screaming at me that this was somehow my doing. Because I don't support this decision at all. You need to finish school. There's plenty of time for you to decide if this is what you want to do."

"I'm pretty sure it is."

"Things can change," he said.

Kaylee decided it wasn't the time to keep pressing him. He seemed pre-occupied, and she had a pretty good idea on what.

She offered to clean up the leftovers as he went to get ready to go out. He came back fifteen minutes later in dark jeans, dark t-shirt, and dark black tactical response jacket he often wore when doing surveillance. Though there was no sign of a printing, Kaylee was sure he was carrying his HK45. He was always good at making sure it never showed.

"We'll talk about this later," he told her as he left.

"Yes, we will," she said, as she pulled out her phone and pulled up the Vegas Metro PD number.

Chapter 42

Mount Charles sat thirty-five miles northeast of Las Vegas. Being part of the Spring Mountain Range, it was the ideal place to escape the AC confines once the heat started soaring well above a hundred.

Roddick wasn't even to his destination when he could feel the cooler air as he drove down Kyle Canyon. Soon the road was enclosed by ascending juniper, Ponderosa pine, and Aspen trees.

Roddick kept going until he turned onto Rainbow Road and reached the general area Mickey had told him the cabin was at. He pulled to the side of the road near a private drive and killed the lights. It wasn't completely dark out, yet Roddick was able to see expensive cars parked at the end of the drive. He spotted a BMW, a Mercedes-Benz, and a Lexus.

The cabin was more of a rustic lodge with a vaulted roof and multiple-level decks. The private lot it sat on was heavily wooded, which made it hard for Roddick to get a good view. He needed to move in closer if he was ever going to see what players were running the Royal Heart Casino.

He opened his camera bag and pulled out his older but trusted model camera. It still had the best stabilizer and zoom than any newer model he'd tested, and it was reliable. You couldn't put a price tag on that.

With one last look on where he needed to go, he

got out and shut the door quietly. To the left of the drive was a thicket of trees and rocks he used as cover as he closed in on the lodge.

The closer he got, the more he could hear talking but he couldn't make out the direction of it. A ridge of uneven ground curled up to the side of the entrance. Roddick opted to army-crawl the rest of the way until he reached the lip of it. From there he had a direct view of the front door.

A tall, short blond-haired man was standing out front, smoking. He had a Slovak look to him with an oval face, compact lips, and pointy nose. When he reached to grab the cigarette from his mouth, it was with a bandaged right hand. More than likely the same hand Dylan Carter's pit bull used as a chew toy.

He zoomed the camera in and got a few snaps off when he felt the barrel of a gun being jammed into his vertebrae.

"Up!"

Still holding the camera, he stood up and raised his arms. The man relieved him of his gun and camera before saying, "Now walk."

The man made Roddick walk to the front, where the Slovak was still smoking his cigarette. He grinned when they came up.

"What did I tell you? Didn't I tell you he vas out zerrre. Take sneaky man inside."

They moved inside, where a group of older, East European men were gathered around in the open living room near a stone fireplace that had an opening large enough to shove an entire pine tree into it. Exposed beams lined the ceiling, connecting with large floor-to-ceiling windows that gave the illusion the native landscape was engulfing you.

Roddick didn't recognize any of the Russian-looking men inside except the fat one sitting comfortably in a leather club chair. It was Boris Sokolov. He was a well-known heroin trafficker and arms dealer. An all-around big man. He stood close to six feet six inches, with hands the size of sausage links, a broad, bloated torso, prominent bald head, and shaggy Rasputin-looking beard.

To see Sokolov did not surprise Roddick. It was who was standing behind Sokolov that did.

"Don't look so surprised, Joe," Toney said.

"Kazimir, see if zerrre is otherrrs," Sokolov said.

Kazimir signaled with his bandaged hand for the man who had held Roddick at gunpoint to come with him. He was shorter than Kazimir, with a shaved head and dark stubble around a slightly plump face. To his side was the shotgun he had jammed into Roddick's back. Both men went out when Roddick turned his attention back to Toney.

"Jesus, Toney, I knew you were dirty but not to this extent."

"You always were too loyal."

"Is he parrrt of ourrr prrroblem?" Sokolov asked

"Who, Joe?" Toney said. "Naw, Joe ain't our problem. Though he's been in contact with him."

Sokolov moved to the edge of the chair and looked directly at Roddick.

"So you have spoken to zis hitman, da?"

"Yes."

"Do you know how to contact him?"

Roddick shook his head. "No."

Sokolov leaned back in his chair, annoyed.

"He is useless to us."

Toney patted Sokolov's shoulder. "Let me fill Joe in on what's going on. He'll be more helpful once he gets that confused look off his face."

Sokolov rolled his yes. "If you must."

Toney stepped toward Roddick. "See, Boris here was one of Carl's clients. He'd come to Vegas once or twice a year. I was assigned to his security, and that's when he started talking about his plans of buying the Lucky Hearts Casino. I told him most of them casinos off The Strip make chump change, and that's when I pitched him the idea of using the casino to launder money."

"Was Shaun involved in this brilliant idea?"

"At first he was, but once shit got real, he bailed."

"Sounds like Shaun," Roddick said.

Toney ignored the remark and continued speaking in a low tone, "So, Boris bought the casino and pretty soon word got around it was the place to go to get rid of your dirty money, and the joint really started making money. That's when Lockhart started feeding Rivera what was going on so they could blackmail us. Boris here thought it best we bring in a professional to clean house. Valentas had a contact at some pawn shop he said could hook us up with one of the best. I didn't know at the time that Lockhart had hired you to find Rivera, or that Rivera's meth head boyfriend both skipped out on Lockhart."

"Were you the one to tell him to come after me?"

"No. It was all Valentas. He arranged it all and is also the one that decided it best to take the hitman out instead of just paying him off."

Roddick wasn't sure how much of that was true or

Toney just pinning it all on a dead man.

"I suppose it was him that also brought in the Armenian muscle."

"That's right. The Armenians use the casino to launder their money so they can buy weapons, and in return, they do jobs for us."

"Like kidnap my daughter and use her as bait?"

"Pretty much," Toney said. "As for the rest, I'm sure you can put it together."

"Right. You got a pissed off professional killer that's picking you off, and you're here hiding, hoping the bad man leaves you alone. That about sum it up?"

Sokolov cursed loud in Russian, which got the other men's attention as they all closed in on him while brandishing their weapons. Toney put his arm up, signaling them to back off.

"I strongly advise you, Joe, not to escalate an already tense situation."

"How did you find us?" Sokolov asked.

"Good question," replied Roddick. "I'd like to answer it but my memory isn't so good on account of being shot in the head."

Sokolov, nor the others in the room liked that answer and made it known by once again starting to move on Roddick.

Toney put his hand up once more to get them to back off.

"You know, Joe, there's only so long I can hold them off."

Approaching headlights shined through one of the windows, providing Roddick a needed distraction as they waited for whoever it was. Roddick could hear talking, and a car door shut followed by approaching footsteps.

Kazimir came in first followed by the shaved-headed goon, who stepped to the side revealing the familiar baby face that belonged to Detective Chase's partner.

"What's he doing here?" McCarthy asked, pointing to Roddick.

"Found sneaky man hiding out front trying to take pictures," Kazimir said, holding up Roddick's camera.

"That so," McCarthy said.

Roddick wasn't so much surprised that Toney was able to find some dirty cops like McCarthy to bring in, but more at the Machiavellianism of it all.

"Kazimir, go back outside and keep guard," Sokolov ordered.

"There's nobody out there, boss."

As Kazimir said this, what first looked like a twirling baton came straight toward the window to the side of him. Glass shattered, and the metal object landed inches from Kazimir's feet. The remaining fuse burnt out before any of them could react. The explosion that came next was deafening as Roddick hit the floor. Pain shot through him as his side tore open from shrapnel, flaying his skin.

His ears rung out as another metal object came through the window. Roddick pressed against the floor as hard as he could to give as little surface area of his body as possible. Another explosion but he could hear nothing. Just the singed smell of gunpowder and flames. Something grabbed his foot. He turned to see Toney crawling up to him. His face was sliced open. He slid a 9mm across the floor for Roddick to grab. Roddick did so and followed Toney to a side wall where McCarthy and the two remaining Russian men had barricaded against.

"It's him," Toney yelled, but Roddick could barely hear him. He turned to look where the first bomb had landed and saw only a smoldering hole in the floor and Kazimir's tore up body beside it.

The shaved-headed man slid to the broken window and started firing buckshot out of it. Several other Russians did the same. They kept firing and reloading like they were at a shooting gallery.

The return fire came hot and heavy. It sprayed across the window like a stream coming out of a garden hose. The shaved-headed man pivoted around as blood poured out of his stomach. More bullets hit his back, and he fell to his knees and flopped over.

The two Russians were hit next and fell almost on top of each other. Roddick saw movement and turned to see Sokolov's fat body crawling along the floor toward them. The firing stopped before anther gyrating metal tube came through the window and hit the ground where it rolled only inches from Sokolov's face.

Roddick closed his eyes but even through his deafness could still hear the earsplitting noise. The cool splash of blood and human matter hit him and he turned away from it.

"We got to get the fuck out of here!" Toney yelled and turned to McCarthy. "Where you parked?"

"Just to the side."

"What about you Joe?"

"Up the drive to the side of the road."

"Give me your keys," Toney yelled, as he pointed a gun at him, so he obliged.

"I'll try and draw his attention while you two go

out the back and get to McCarthy's car. Soon as you get going, he'll come gunning for you, and I'll slip out and take Joe's car."

They all nodded and Roddick followed McCarthy to the back while Toney crawled to the window and took one of the fallen Russian's shotguns.

The house was full of smoke with small fires burning parts of the wooden floor and furniture. It was hard to navigate but Roddick kept behind McCarthy until they reached a small door near the kitchen. They got out just as Toney started firing.

The fresh, cooler air got Roddick out of his temporary daze but his ears were still ringing. They rounded the corner to see the Nissan Maxima parked to the side. McCarthy crawled to the driver's side door and slowly opened it. Roddick followed suit and slid into the passenger side. McCarthy lay crouched down in the seat for a moment, trying to catch his breath before sticking the key in the ignition.

The moment the starter turned over bullets were bouncing off the back of the car. McCarthy punched the accelerator hard and jerked the wheel almost a full 90-degree rotation so the radiator was now pointed to the way out.

With their path cleared, McCarthy floored it. The roar of rubber tearing into loose gravel was followed by automatic gunfire. The stream of bullets sheared the side of the car and McCarthy along with it.

Roddick tried to grab the wheel, but it was too late. The Maxima veered hard right and wrapped around a ponderosa pine. The hood crumpled up like Origami paper into the windshield as impact deployed both the driver and passenger dash airbags. Roddick's head hit the airbag hard enough to nearly knock him unconscious.

"No," a voice kept telling Roddick. "Not again. Wake up!" His eyes felt like they were cemented shut, but he tried all he could to open them again. "If you don't open them you won't wake up this time."

With his eyes now slightly ajar, the blurring image of a man in what looked like tactical gear leaning over him.

Come to finish me off.

Somehow through his impaired hearing, he heard his own car starting from up the drive. The blurred figure turned away from him and started firing.

Though he remained awake upon further recall, Roddick couldn't remember anything else. Just the sound of sirens.

Chapter 43

There was a sandstorm advisory out, but it didn't stop Detective Chase from his motorcycle excursion into the desert.

The sky was darkening, and the winds were picking up to over thirty miles an hour, but he kept going. It had been a long week around the clock, questioning by his sergeant, Lieutenant Cervantes, and the police chief. At first, they didn't believe he didn't know about McCarthy's involvement with the Russians and the Lucky Hearts Casino.

When Kaylee had called and gave him directions to some meeting near Mt. Charleston, Chase had a feeling it was about to be blown open. But he had no idea to the extent until he got there. Reports of massive gunfire had brought in a cavalry of responding officers. The lodge was shot to hell and starting to burn from the explosive devices that were set off inside.

He was becoming accustomed to the sort of mayhem the Scorpion brought with him, but nothing could have prepared him for seeing the Nissan Maxima he shared with McCarthy wrapped around a tree. McCarthy was already dead when he got there, and Roddick was barely conscious as he mumbled gibberish from the passenger seat.

The medics got to Roddick before he could really question him. But he had a good idea who the main culprit was. It was all too similar to the villa massacre.

Things unfolded fast in the following days. Roddick gave details from the hospital about what happened, and it seemed to match the evidence and bodies that were identified. All confirmed Russian and foreign criminals via INTERPOL databases, the biggest being Sokolov.

Warrants were granted fast, and local police and Feds turned the Lucky Hearts Casino upside down. Any remaining staff that might have actually known anything had already fled to Russia, and little was turned up.

No matter, the casino was closed and the likelihood of it ever re-opening under its current management was none. It'd be dynamited to the ground within a year and another casino would pop up in its place. That was how these types of things were handled in Vegas.

The same kind of mindset applied to the investigation. Most of his hitman's kills were pinned on Kazimir, who fit the vague physical description given of Chase's killer..

As for the main perp who did all the killing at the cabin, it was assumed it was one of Toney's accomplices and they had both fled the scene together and were still at large.

It was bullshit, they knew it was, but they were okay with it as long as the media bought it, which they did. The entire thing was out of the national headlines within days and Metro PD was praised for the swiftness of the investigation. More importantly, back to business as usual. Keep feeding those slots. There's nothing to worry about.

Soon as he was cleared of any involvement, Chase

was put on immediate paid leave. He knew why. So he would have plenty of time to cool his head and really think twice about going against the narrative they laid out. It was damage control on their end with McCarthy's involvement.

The way the police spokesman spun it, McCarthy was your typical loose cannon that went against the department. So his involvement, for the most part, was glossed over by the juicier international crime aspect of the story.

Chase throttled up and swerved past a jack rabbit that jumped in front of his front tire before making a sharp turn onto a gravel fire road. A few miles down was a lone wooden outhouse with a crescent moon cut in the door. Next to it was a leaning, single telephone pole held up only by a strand of guy-wire.

The road got rougher from there as his tires bounced from the rocky wash. He aimed for the larger rocks to ride over and kept a steady speed until one of the rocks skidded out from under him. The RPMs spiked as he hit his side hard and felt a sharp pain in his shoulder when the weight of the bike fell on top of him.

He stayed on his side several minutes, trying to move past the pain, before pushing the bike off him. Back on his feet, Chase rotated his bruised shoulder until it loosened up. The sky was darkening even more, while behind him a wall of dust could be seen. He didn't pay attention to it as he started the bike up and kept going. He knew what was behind him.

****

The enclosed courtyard of Plaza Guadalajara was crowded. A small shopping mall built in the traditional Spanish colonial design and painted in bright yellow.

Many of the patrons were American who crossed the border to Los Algodones for the cheap dental, vision, and prescription drugs that cost pennies on the dollar.

Toney sat at an empty table under the shade and people watched while nursing his fourth beer of the afternoon. He had nothing else to do. He'd gotten to the border town in under five hours in Roddick's car. From there, he ditched the car at the Quechan Indian tribe parking lot adjacent to the border checkpoint and walked across.

He had cleared out his bank accounts before leaving Vegas but he needed more. He took a room and slept most of the day. Once he had woken, then eaten from one of the many taco trucks in the park, he got hold of a contact who had salted away a good chunk of his money. It would take a few days for the money to be wired to him. After that, who knew? Maybe somewhere in the butt crack of South America? He always did like Brazilian women.

He thought about Mikaela. He saw online that she had canceled the remainder of her Vegas shows to focus on her next album. He wondered if the police had found out about them and put her through the wringer about his whereabouts. Maybe when he settled down at wherever he decided to go, he'd send word to her.

He left the Plaza and walked around town. It was nothing but endless dentist offices and pharmacies. He passed through the stretch of tents and sidewalk vendors selling everything from t-shirts, blankets, Talavera pottery, to even their own children.

Dirty, junk cars sat parked while feral cats slept under them for shade from the brutal sun. Toney stopped at a smoke shop and bought a couple cigars and a plug of tobacco that he sliced a chunk off with his pocket knife. He spat the juice out along Avenue B and looked up at the city water tower, half smiling at its welcoming sign in the distance.

He continued to wander along until the street connected to Calle 2 and went in the direction of the town's well-known house of tolerance.

He'd been a regular customer since he arrived over a week ago. It was an old hotel with a catacomb of rooms you could rent out for a certain amount of time. All the prostitutes were required to have up-to-date health certificates so they were cleaner than women you would have one-nighters with in the big city.

The place was run by a fat Mexican Madam named Camila Trujillo. She always dressed in a traditional ankle-length skirt with flowers on it and a blouse with pockets. She'd been known in her younger years to carry rocks in those pockets and stand out on one of the room balconies and thrown them at overzealous clergymen and their meat axes.

Two beefy Vaquero boys guarded the front door. They always stood there with their thumbs in their belt, joking with each other while catcalling the white women that would walk by.

The one that spoke English was Francisco. He did irrigation work in the morning and watched the door in the afternoon.

"Señor Frank," he said, when he saw Toney. Frank was the fake name he had given out. He was using several of them. At the hotel, he was registered under Anton.

"Damn hot today," Toney said

"Si, it is. You take it easy in there today, eh,

amigo? Don't want to overheat."

Toney laughed and went in. Trujillo was in the back parlor room with several of the girls. They were putting a jigsaw puzzle together and drinking whiskey. She looked up when she saw Toney and a cigar in one of his outreached hands.

"Señor Frank. Gracias," she said, taking it. He lit it for her and watched as she puffed on it and nodded in approval.

"One of the girls?" she asked.

Toney nodded.

"For how long?"

"Just an hour this time."

Frank often kept them overnight but only paid for a few hours, which angered Trujillo. He'd gotten her the cigar as a peace offering.

"Si, si. Upstairs, second room. I'll send a girl up shortly."

Toney grinned and started up. His smile vanished as soon as he opened the second door on the left. Standing just inside was an average-sized blondish man.

"The Candyman," the Scorpion said.

Toney saw the Glock pointed at him and raised his hands as he stepped into the room.

"Look. It wasn't me that double-crossed you. It was Valentas, and you already took care of him. How'd you find me?"

"Does it matter?"

"Yes."

"You had the misfortune of ditching one car I had a tracker on and taking another. It didn't take much time finding you. It's a small town."

"I got money being wired to me soon. A lot. If you just—"

The shot hit him square between the eyes. He took a back step toward the doorway before his legs gave out. He flopped for a few seconds on the floor like a flailing fish and then nothing.

Francisco and the other man ran up and looked at Toney's body. Francisco smiled, and both men took a leg and dragged Toney out.

****

Kaylee couldn't sleep. It was her first week back in her dorm for the start of the fall term. The only sleep she did get was from the Valium. She worried about her dad.

A former homicide detective now content doing mindless workers' comp and insurance claims. Each time she saw him he seemed more checked out. He didn't play pool with her anymore. Or invite her to sporting events. If he wasn't at the office he was in front of the TV drinking beer.

She thought about all the times when he was in the coma, she would sit by his side wishing for him to wake up. And when he did, she thought it had come true, but in actuality, it turned out to be a monkey paw wish. For only a small part of him really woke up that day.

She turned to her side and thought about him. As much as she tried, she couldn't think about her dad without the Scorpion cropping up.

She'd sent a text to the number she had for him asking for him to call, but so far he hadn't. And that was weeks ago. He was gone, and it infuriated her. The death and pain he had left in his wake meant nothing. On to another destination and bringing death and broken lives with him.

She cursed. No matter how long it took, someday she was going to find him. He was not going to be able to stay out of range forever.

A word about the author...

Grant Bywaters has worked as a licensed private investigator and holds a B.S. in psychology from Portland State University. Bywaters lives outside of Portland, Oregon.

Thank you for purchasing
this publication of The Wild Rose Press, Inc.

For questions or more information
contact us at
info@thewildrosepress.com.

The Wild Rose Press, Inc.
www.thewildrosepress.com